W9-CIC-322

SNOWBOARD SHOWDOWN

READ ALL THE BOOKS

In The

New MATT CHRISTOPHER Sports Library!

CATCH THAT PASS!
978-1-59953-105-2

CENTER COURT STING
978-1-59953-106-9

DIRT BIKE RACER
978-1-59953-113-7

ICE MAGIC
978-1-59953-112-0

THE KID WHO ONLY HIT HOMERS
978-1-59953-107-6

LONG ARM QUARTERBACK
978-1-59953-114-4

MOUNTAIN BIKE MANIA
978-1-59953-108-3

SKATEBOARD TOUGH
978-1-59953-115-1

SNOWBOARD MAVERICK
978-1-59953-116-8

SNOWBOARD SHOWDOWN
978-1-59953-109-0

SOCCER HALFBACK
978-1-59953-110-6

SOCCER SCOOP
978-1-59953-117-5

The New

Sports Library

SNOWBOARD
SHOWDOWN

NORWOOD HOUSE PRESS

CHICAGO, ILLINOIS

Norwood House Press
P.O. Box 316598
Chicago, Illinois 60631

For information regarding Norwood House Press, please visit our website at:
www.norwoodhousepress.com or call 866-565-2900.

This edition was published in 2007.

Library of Congress Cataloging-in-Publication Data:
Mantell, Paul.
  Snowboard showdown.
     p. cm. -- (The new Matt Christopher sports library)
  Summary: Rivalry flares between twelve-year-old Freddie and his
fourteen-year-old brother Dondi, both on and off the snowboarding slopes,
nearly leading to disaster.
  ISBN-13: 978-1-59953-109-0 (library : alk. paper)
  ISBN-10: 1-59953-109-7 (library : alk. paper)
1. Large type books. (1. Snowboarding--Fiction. 2. Brothers--Fiction. 3.
Large type books.) I. Title.
  PZ7.C458Sn 2007
  (Fic)--dc22

                                        2006036349

Printed in the United States of America

To John Carson

SNOWBOARD
SHOWDOWN

Freddie Ruiz tightened the straps on his snow-board, securing his feet into position. He fastened the leash to his calf so his board wouldn't go flying while he was airborne. He took a few deep breaths of the biting, cold air and lowered his tinted goggles over his eyes to protect them from the glare of the snow.

"Here I come, Dondi!" he shouted to his brother, who was waiting at the bottom of the halfpipe's gentle slope. Moments before, Dondi had successfully executed a series of moves that Freddie was going to try to match.

The two boys were playing their own version of Pig, where a player adds a letter of the word *pig* for each time he fails to match a run. Whoever got *pig* first was the loser. So far, Freddie had a *p,* and Dondi had a *pi.*

Freddie, at twelve, was a seventh-grader at Crestview Middle School while Dondi, fourteen, was in eighth grade. But even though Freddie was eighteen months younger, and smaller, their competitions often ended with Freddie's winning. Dondi might be better at most things, but Freddie was definitely a better athlete.

"You're going to choke!" Dondi taunted Freddie.

Freddie clenched his fists and bit his lip to keep from answering back. He would answer with a perfect run. That was the best way to get back at Dondi.

He turned his body and board downhill. Slowly, the board slid down the snowy slope. When he had gained enough speed, Freddie leaned to the right, heading up the wall. *Whoosh!* He took the air then twisted left in a 180° turn. He landed perfectly, still moving at top speed.

Now he was riding fakie, with the tail of his board forward, back down the wall. He stared straight ahead, trying not to look at the drop ahead of him. He ran up the other wall and hit the top, then launched himself into the air again in imitation of Dondi's second jump. He twisted, uncoiling like a spring, and paused to grab his board, his free hand high in the air behind him. He felt dizzy as he came down, and he wobbled for a moment. But he righted himself just in time, barely touching the snow with his left hand.

Now he went into his third and final move. Coming up the wall, he held his breath. This was a difficult move. Dondi had never done it successfully before today. Freddie had to nail it now or get an *i*. If he let Dondi win this match, he'd never hear the end of it.

At the very top of the wall, Freddie twisted left, letting the board circle with him, and did a full 360° turn. He landed perfectly and slid easily down the slope, fists raised high, to where his brother stood waiting.

"Ha!" Freddie shouted in triumph as he skidded to a stop. "In your face, dude!"

Dondi shook his head, his long dark hair held in place by the headband he wore all the time. "You missed the second move," he said flatly, crossing his arms with finality.

"I did not!" Freddie retorted, his voice rising to a squeaky pitch.

"Did too," Dondi insisted. "I saw your hand hit the snow."

"I just grazed it," Freddie replied. "It was a good move."

"You blew the move."

"Did not, you jerk!" Freddie tried to move toward Dondi, but he'd forgotten he was still strapped to his board. He fell face first into the snow. As he pushed himself up again, he heard Dondi's mocking laughter.

"Nice move, dweeb!" Dondi said. "That was a ten plus."

"Shut up," Freddie grumbled, unstrapping his feet.

"Make me," Dondi said, motioning for Freddie to come at him.

"I will," Freddie said. Springing up, he flew at Dondi, knocking him backward into the snow. The two brothers wrestled furiously, rolling over and over, fists flying but mostly missing — until Dondi caught Freddie in the nose.

"Ow!" Freddie yelled. "Ow, ow, ow!" Drops of

blood reddened the snow beneath his head. "You broke my nose!"

"It's not broken, stupid," Dondi scowled, taking off his gloves. He reached into his coat pocket and pulled out a wad of tissues. "It's just a little blood. It's nothing. Here, use this. It'll be fine in a minute."

"Leave me alone," Freddie said, fighting back tears. He grabbed the tissues, held them to his nose, and turned his back on his brother.

"Okay, okay, I'll leave you alone," Dondi muttered. "Sorry about the bloody nose. It was an accident."

"It was not," Freddie shot back. "And I'm telling Papi."

"Fine. Tell him," Dondi said. "You started it anyway."

"I did not!" Freddie screeched.

"'I did not!'" Dondi mimicked.

"Shut up before I kill you!" Freddie shouted.

"Oh, I'm really scared of a pipsqueak like you," Dondi said. "Anyway, that's *p-i* for you. So now we're even."

"It is not," Freddie argued. "I don't want to play anymore."

"Fine. Quitter," Dondi said with a shrug. "I win by default."

"Do not."

"Do too."

Just then, a car horn beeped in the parking lot behind them. "Papi's here," Dondi said. "You'd better not make up a story about your nose."

"Yeah, right," Freddie said, checking his nose to see if the bleeding had stopped. It had, but Freddie was still feeling bitter. "How about I just show him these bloody tissues and see what he says?"

"Sure, go ahead. That's your whole life, getting me into trouble," Dondi said, a touch of anger in his voice. "You're a little tattletale."

"I am not!"

"And you're a quitter, too," Dondi persisted. "If you weren't, you'd go back up there and try to beat me fair and square."

"I'm not going to keep Papi waiting," Freddie said.

"Why not?" Dondi asked, staring off into the distance. "He's got nothing better to do."

Freddie steamed. Their dad had lost his job a few months earlier. Dondi never lost an opportunity to comment about it behind his back.

Freddie glanced at his watch. Their father was ten minutes early. Surely he wouldn't mind if the boys took one more run? "Okay," Freddie said, heading up the hill. "Just to show you who's better."

This time down the hill, Freddie started out in fakie position and did a backside 180° indy, grabbing the board and using his hand to turn it in midair. He repeated the move three times, nailing it each time, knowing Dondi stood no chance of landing it even once. He reached the bottom and skidded to a stop right in front of — his father.

"Freddie," Esteban Ruiz said. "Why didn't you come when I beeped for you? I don't have time to sit around and wait for you."

"Sorry, Papi," Freddie said, staring at the snow. "But Dondi —"

"And don't start blaming everything on your brother," his father cut in. "This is between me and you. When I call you, you're supposed to come right away."

"I know, Papi," Freddie said. "But —"

"No buts. Get that board off and let's go. Dondi's already in the car."

Freddie silently removed the board from his feet,

tucked it under his arm, and trudged through the snow behind his father. Dondi had outwitted him again. He had probably run straight for the car the minute Freddie started climbing the hill.

The old station wagon was idling in the parking lot, its windows fogged over. Dondi sat in the back-seat, hunkered down with a sly smile on his face. Freddie got in beside him and slammed the door. He shot Dondi a hateful look, but Dondi didn't return it.

The sun had gone down and Esteban put on the headlights. He drove carefully through the hilly, icy roads. The town of Crestview was nestled in the foothills of the Santa Elena Mountains. There were many ski resorts within an hour's drive of town, and in winter most of the kids who were old enough could be found skiing, skating, or snowboarding somewhere in the hills and mountains.

Dondi and Freddie had started skiing when they were very little. And a few years later, when snow-boarding came along, they were two of the first kids to try it. Right away, both Dondi and Freddie had taken to the sport. At first, Freddie was the better of the two. He was a natural at boarding, as he was at

8

all sports. But Dondi soon caught up to him, thanks to his longer skiing experience. He was six inches taller than Freddie and more muscular, too, due to a recent growth spurt. Freddie remained small and skinny. It wasn't long before they began competing against each other on the slopes.

In fact, it seemed that Freddie and Dondi never missed a chance to compete. Even silly things — who was going to get the bigger portion of dessert, who could shovel more snow out of the driveway, who could do the best imitation of their favorite TV characters — became contests. Often, verbal battles turned into physical ones. Today's bloody nose was a typical result of their more recent tussles.

This tendency to fight drove both their parents up the wall. With Esteban at home searching for a new job and Aida working longer hours than usual, the burden of keeping the peace fell mostly on their dad these days. That was the last thing his dad needed, Freddie knew. Esteban was depressed about losing his job of fifteen years, even though it hadn't been his fault. Breaking up constant arguments between his sons only made him more depressed. Freddie tried to stay out of fights, for his dad's sake — but

9

with Dondi, that was next to impossible. Like right now, for instance.

"Get your leg off me!" Freddie growled, shoving Dondi's leg away. The leg had gradually crept across the backseat and had ended up on top of Freddie's.

"I'm bigger than you. I need more space." Dondi stretched theatrically. "It's not fair. Why can't I sit up front?"

"Because I don't want you fiddling with the radio," Esteban said, glancing at Dondi in the rearview mirror. "I don't like the way you just reach over and turn that junky music up so loud. It hurts my ears."

"It's not junky music!" Dondi said. "You just don't have any taste."

Freddie burned with anger. "Don't talk to Papi like that," he said.

"Shut up, squirt," Dondi said. "I'll talk any way I want."

"Boys, stop it, both of you!" Esteban said. "I'm driving the car, and the roads are slippery. You want to cause an accident?"

Freddie looked daggers at Dondi. Dondi's lips

mouthed, *I'll get you later.* Freddie looked away, struggling to keep his fury in check.

Dondi is such a big mouth, Freddie thought as he stared out into the darkness. Why did he have to be that way, anyway? Why couldn't he have been the kind of brother other kids had?

The car pulled into the driveway, and they all piled out. "Don't start fighting again," their dad warned them. "I've had a tough enough day already."

Freddie wondered what his dad meant, but he didn't ask. If Papi wanted to talk about what was bothering him, Freddie would listen, for sure. But right now, nobody felt like talking.

Freddie's nose hurt, and he was bone-tired. He trudged up the stairs to his room and threw himself down on the bed to rest.

2

Freddie's mother worked at a software company in Riverhead, forty-five minutes away. These days she never got home before six o'clock. At five-thirty, Freddie heard Esteban in the kitchen, pulling down cans from the pantry shelves.

Freddie frowned. His dad wasn't much of a cook and didn't seem interested in learning how to become one, either. Freddie wasn't going to complain, but he knew Dondi would. Another of Dondi's "wonderful" qualities, Freddie reflected sadly.

"Hey, squirt." Freddie looked up to see his brother staring at him from the doorway.

"Get out of my room," Freddie said immediately.

"Come on, forgive and forget," Dondi said, coming into the room and sitting on the edge of Freddie's bed.

"I said get out!" Freddie said, his voice rising to a shout.

"Shhh, quiet! You want to get Papi upset?" Dondi said.

Freddie felt like screaming. Dondi always did that, played innocent when he was really the cause of all the trouble. But he was right about one thing — Freddie didn't want to upset his father. Downstairs, he could hear the blender going. Good. No way he would have heard Freddie shout.

"I'm sorry about your nose, okay?" Dondi said. "Come on, it was just one of those things."

"No, it wasn't."

"Okay, it wasn't," Dondi admitted, a sly grin appearing on his handsome face. His black eyes sparkled, and he reached back and flipped his ponytail off his neck. "Come on, get over it."

"I would have beaten you today, and you know it," Freddie said.

"Sure you would have," Dondi said, his smile widening. "Sure. Right."

"You could never do that reverse-indy move, Dondi," Freddie insisted.

"I can do anything you can, and double," Dondi

said. "Cueball." Dondi put a hand on Freddie's buzz cut and rubbed it.

That did it. "Cut it out!" Freddie yelled, knocking Dondi's hand away.

"When are you getting a haircut, anyway?" Dondi asked, getting up. "You're looking shaggy."

"Shut up!" Freddie screeched. "You're the one who needs a haircut. You look like a girl with that ponytail."

"What did you call me?" Dondi asked, suddenly angry. He came at Freddie, shoving him with his hands. "Take it back, squirt."

In moments, they were at each other again. Dondi pounded Freddie with a pillow. Freddie kicked out, scoring once with a hit to Dondi's knee, which only made Dondi fight harder. He covered Freddie's face with the pillow and pushed down hard before letting go.

Freddie shot up and stood on the bed, gasping for breath. "Papi!" he called at the top of his lungs. "Dondi tried to kill me!"

"I did not!" Dondi yelled. "I was just getting him back!"

Esteban pounded up the stairs. "You boys are going to stop this nonsense right now!" he demanded.

"He started it!" Freddie said hotly. "He came into my room! And" — Freddie cast a glance at Dondi — "he gave me a bloody nose earlier."

"He what?" Esteban turned to Dondi, who was glaring at his brother.

"It was an accident!" Dondi insisted.

"Was not!"

"Whoa!" Esteban brought them both to silence with one firm wave of his hand. "Look, you two boys are supposed to be brothers. When are you going to start acting like it?"

"I came in here to make up," Dondi said softly.

"He walked right in here without being invited," Freddie pointed out.

Suddenly Esteban sighed. He sat down on the bed with a deflated look on his face. "I guess I didn't do such a good job raising you two," he said, shaking his head. "I tried to teach you about sportsmanship, and standing up for each other, not tearing each other down. But I guess I didn't get through to you."

Freddie looked at his father, then quickly dropped

his gaze. Guilt washed over him. Esteban had gone from angry to depressed in a matter of seconds, and Freddie knew he was partly to blame. He was about to apologize when Dondi cut him off.

"Papi," Dondi said with an injured voice, "I can't help it. Everything I do annoys him. It's like, if I hum a tune, he tells me to shut up, and if I come into his room, he yells at me."

Freddie felt like punching his brother. All of a sudden, Dondi was the big victim, and Freddie was the monster. Like Dondi hadn't done anything to make him angry in the first place. Yeah, right.

"Dondi, you're the big brother," Esteban said. "You're supposed to take good care of Freddie. Be someone he can look up to."

"It's not fair!" Dondi protested. "Why do I always have to give in, never him? Just because he's younger?"

"Donovan," Esteban said, using his son's full name as he did only in certain moments, "it's just by chance that you happen to be older. But it means you've got certain responsibilities. I expect you to live up to the job."

"Oh, you want me to do my job?" Dondi suddenly

16

changed from victim to attacker. "How about you do *your* job? You're supposed to be the father around here. Why don't you start acting like one?"

"Dondi —"

"No, I want to know. Why don't you go get a job so Mami can be home more? She wouldn't let Freddie get away with everything the way you do!"

Without another look at either Freddie or his father, Dondi stormed out of the room and slammed the door behind him.

3

I don't know what it is," Freddie said to his best friend, Eric Schwartz, as he pushed Eric's wheelchair down the school hallway toward the cafeteria. Eric was perfectly capable of wheeling his own chair. But the school hallways were narrow, and since they had to walk single file anyway, Freddie had slung his book bag over his shoulders and offered to push.

"Why does he always have to start with me?" Freddie wondered aloud.

"I know what it is," Eric replied, looking back over his shoulder. "He's jealous of you."

"Jealous? Are you kidding me? Why should he be jealous?"

"Because you're a better athlete than he is — isn't it obvious?" Eric was always saying that everything

18

was obvious. Maybe to him it was, with his straight-A average. But to Freddie, Dondi's behavior was one big mystery.

"You think so? He's faster than me in track."

"Yeah, but that's only because his legs are longer. A couple years from now, you'll beat him at that, too."

"Hmm." Freddie smiled at the thought of it. He knew that sooner or later, he was going to start growing in leaps and bounds. He'd been two inches longer at birth than Dondi, and the doctors were always telling his mom that Freddie would be taller as a grown-up. But for now, it was really irritating to be the smaller, skinnier brother.

"I'll tell you one thing," Freddie said as they entered the noisy cafeteria, "I'm never going snowboarding with him again. He always wants to play Pig, but when I beat him, it always makes him mad. What's the point?"

Eric heaved a sigh. "I wish I could go snowboarding with you," he said.

Freddie pushed Eric toward the tables, looking for a place to sit. "Yeah. I wish you could too."

Eric had been in a wheelchair ever since a car had

hit him when he was six. He made the best of it, though. No one could say that Eric Schwartz wasted time feeling sorry for himself, Freddie reflected with pride. Eric was proof positive that you didn't have to dance or play sports or even walk to be popular. He had been elected president of the seventh-grade student council that September, by a huge margin. Freddie couldn't think of a single person who didn't like Eric — even Dondi.

"Hi, Freddie," came a girl's voice from one of the tables as they passed. "Hi, Eric."

Freddie didn't need to turn to find out whose voice it was — it was Clarissa Logan's. Freddie had had a major crush on her ever since sixth grade when she'd suddenly grown from a skinny little kid to a willowy, beautiful girl with dark, wavy hair and long lashes shading big green eyes.

Freddie had a hard time not staring at her whenever they were in the same room together. He'd actually joined chorus because he knew she'd be in it. A couple of times, the music teacher had singled him out for not paying attention. Worse, Clarissa had even caught him staring once. He'd looked away immediately, but he knew she'd seen him.

From the corner of his eye, he caught her cover her mouth to stifle a giggle. Freddie wasn't sure if she was laughing at him or because she liked him. But he felt himself go red all over anyway.

He'd promised himself to be cool around her from then on. When the Thanksgiving dance had come around, he hadn't been able to get up the nerve to ask her, and she'd gone with someone else — an eighth-grader. And why not? Freddie thought. Clarissa Logan sure looked like an eighth-grader herself. And him? He looked like a sixth-grader, at best. When, oh, when, was he going to start growing?

"Hi," he murmured, slowing to a halt. He'd meant to keep going, but Eric and Clarissa started talking about a math test they'd both taken that morning. Freddie stood awkwardly, waiting for them to finish.

"You guys want to join us?" Clarissa asked. "Girls, shove over, okay?"

Freddie looked down at Eric. "You want to?" he asked.

"Sure. You?"

"I guess." Trying to seem nonchalant, Freddie sat down next to Clarissa. As he did, he bumped her elbow. Freddie drew back as if he'd touched fire, stammered an apology.

The table was crowded with other kids Freddie knew, all busy talking with one another. Smart Krissie from French class, and Kareem the computer wizard, and tall Oliver, the star of the basketball team.

"I was wondering," Clarissa asked Eric, continuing their conversation about the math test, "if you understood the part about the slopes and meridians. Midterms are coming up and I don't know what I'm doing."

"Well," Eric said, "it's not that complicated really. I could help you study sometime if you want."

"Really? Cool!" Clarissa said with a dazzling smile.

Freddie squirmed. Eric was so up front, so out there. He'd practically asked Clarissa out, and she'd pretty much said yes, while Freddie just sat there, too shy to say anything. On the other hand, maybe Eric was just being friendly, and Clarissa was just being friendly back. Maybe . . .

"I could use a lesson on that stuff too," Freddie blurted out. "Maybe I could join you?" He knew he was horning in, but he'd opened his mouth before he could stop himself.

Before Clarissa and Eric could say anything, Dondi appeared over Clarissa's shoulder.

"Hey, squirt," Dondi said, nodding to Freddie.

Freddie glared at him, reddening. In two seconds, with two simple words, Dondi had humiliated him in front of his best friend and the girl he had a major crush on. Boy, was that ever Dondi. "What do you want?" he asked Dondi.

"Guess what? I got my working papers!" He held them up for the whole table to see. "Anybody wanna hire me? Only fifty dollars an hour!" Everyone laughed at Dondi's clowning, as everyone always did. Dondi never seemed to get embarrassed or worry that he'd said or done something wrong — take now, for instance. It was like he was a stand-up comic or something. Freddie wished he could be like that, but whenever he tried to be funny, it usually came out wrong. So he didn't try to be funny much anymore.

"Wow, that is so awesome!" Clarissa said enthusiastically, handling Dondi's working papers as if they were made of diamonds. "I wish I could get a job.

Something cool. Like Mabry's, where they sell all those great clothes." She looked up at Dondi admiringly.

"I'm gonna get you a special discount if you come in to where I work," Dondi promised.

"I am so there!" Clarissa told Dondi, and they slapped each other five. Then, to Freddie's horror, Dondi winked at her.

"Y-you don't even have a job yet," Freddie blurted out, stumbling over the words. He wanted to take the working papers and crush them into a ball. Instead, he handed them back to Dondi.

"I will by tonight, you wait and see," Dondi told him. Then he sauntered off, pointing meaningfully at Clarissa, who giggled.

Suddenly, Freddie felt like he was drowning. He stood up, using the table for support. "I . . . gotta go," he said, grabbing his book bag and waving a quick good-bye. "See ya."

He broke into a trot as he neared the exit doors, then stopped and leaned against a wall in the stairwell. He breathed deeply, trying to collect himself. Had Dondi flirted with Clarissa just because he suspected Freddie liked her? But how would he know?

Not even Eric knew Freddie liked Clarissa. But why else would Dondi have paid any attention to a seventh-grader?

One thing was for sure: If Freddie wanted to get Clarissa to like him, he was going to have to get her attention away from Dondi first.

The rest of that day, Freddie couldn't stop thinking about Dondi and Clarissa. He imagined Clarissa coming into the place where Dondi worked. It was painful to imagine them together.

Well, he consoled himself, maybe Dondi wouldn't get a job. After all, not many people were willing to hire fourteen-year-olds. And if he did get a job, it probably would be something nasty, like taking out smelly garbage from restaurant kitchens. Freddie chuckled at the thought of Clarissa coming to visit Dondi at his job and being grossed out because he smelled like rotting garbage.

But no such luck. That evening, Dondi burst into the kitchen, his fists raised in triumph and a big smug smile plastered all over his face.

"Guess what — I got a job!" he crowed. "Say hello to the working dude, here. Yes! I am the man!"

25

Aida Ruiz rose from her chair to embrace her son. "My baby! That's fantastic!" she cried.

"*Bueno,* Donovan. I'm proud of you," Esteban said lightly. "Come, sit down, let's eat, and you'll tell us all about it."

They sat down, and Dondi launched into his story. "I couldn't believe it — I figured I'd have to go into half a dozen places before I found something. But I happened to go straight to Buddy's, first thing, 'cause I wanted to check out this excellent snowboard."

Buddy's Sporting Goods was Freddie's favorite store in all of Crestview. He had bought his baseball mitt there, and his Rollerblades and hockey stick, and his soccer ball, and his tennis racket.

"And I see this sign in the window saying they're hiring part-time, and I figured, Well, that's me, so I go up to the guy and show him my working papers, and he remembers me because I'm in there a lot, so he hires me! Is that awesome or what?"

Dondi's eyes were sparkling with joy. "And guess what else? I get to buy anything in the store at a special employee bargain price! Man, I'm gonna get me some gooood stuff!" He clapped his hands delightedly and dug into his food. "I'm gonna buy you something too, squirt, you'll see," he told Freddie. "Something you'll like."

Freddie was startled. Evidently, Dondi was in such a good mood that he'd decided he could afford to be nice to his brother.

"So what do you say?" Dondi prodded, leaning forward.

"Thank you," Freddie mumbled, knowing that was what his parents were expecting him to say. Sure enough, he caught them smiling at each other. They did that whenever Dondi and Freddie were getting along.

Enjoy it now, Freddie thought ruefully. Dondi will never get me anything. We'll be sworn enemies again before too long, I'm sure.

Freddie was in social studies class a few afternoons later when his friend Steve Myers leaned over and whispered in his ear, "Your brother has been dissing me around."

Freddie's eyes widened. "Really? What'd he say?"

"Tell you after class," Steve said, eyeing the teacher, Ms. Raven, who was turning in their direction.

Once the bell had rung and the two boys were gathering their books, Freddie said, "Tell me. What'd he say?"

"He's been telling everybody in school that I don't know how to snowboard," Steve said, his mouth twisting into a grimace.

"Dondi's a jerk," Freddie said sympathetically. "It's not like he's so great himself, either."

"I know!" Steve said as they went out into the hallway. "He acts like he's all that, but he isn't that much better than me. And you're much better than he is, Freddie."

"Yeah, well, so what?" Freddie asked glumly. "What good does that do me?"

"Huh?"

Freddie sighed. "Oh, nothing. Forget Dondi. I try to," Freddie said. "We could go out to the halfpipe after school."

"Cool!" Steve said, brightening. "You could show me some fresh moves and maybe tell me what I'm doing wrong."

"You don't necessarily have to be doing something wrong," Freddie commented. "Dondi could just be trying to push your buttons. He does that to me all the time."

"What if he's there?" Steve asked, suddenly anxious.

"Relax, he won't be there," Freddie assured him. "He's got a job after school now. At Buddy's."

"At Buddy's? Man, he is so lucky!" Steve said, a look of envy on his face.

Coming toward him in the hallway, Freddie saw

Clarissa wheeling Eric. "Hey, you guys," Freddie greeted them. "We're going out to the halfpipe this afternoon. You want to come and watch?"

"Can't," Eric said. "I've got to do my science project."

"You didn't do that yet?" Steve asked. "How can you leave it to the last minute like that?"

"He can," Freddie assured him. "He'll get an A, too. He always does. I could punch him, he's so smart."

Freddie turned to Clarissa. "How 'bout you, Clarissa? Want to come snowboarding?" Freddie asked hopefully.

"No, sorry," she said. "I've never gone snowboarding."

"Really? Maybe I could —"

"Anyway, I can't," she interrupted him. "I'm going to the mall."

Freddie gulped. "The mall?" he repeated.

"Yeah," she said, giving them all a captivating smile. "Dondi invited me to come visit him at his new job. He said he'd buy me a sundae at Barlow's. Can't resist that," she said.

The second bell rang. "Dang, we're late," Eric said.

"Come on, Clarissa. See you guys later!" Clarissa began pushing the wheelchair, and the two of them were off.

"We'd better get to study hall," Steve said to Freddie. "Hey. What's the matter with you? You look like you just got bad news or something."

"I did," Freddie said.

"Huh? Oh, I get it," Steve said knowingly as the truth dawned on him. "You like Clarissa, huh? Man, get in line. Half the guys in school like her."

"Thanks for sharing that, Steve," he said. "Besides, she likes Dondi, so I can forget about it."

"Come on," Steve said as they entered the auditorium for study hall. "How could she like him better than you?"

"Well, let's see now," Freddie said. "He's an eighth-grader, he's got a job, he knows how to act with girls . . . want me to go on?"

"At least you're better at snowboarding," Steve offered lamely.

"Yeah. Great." Freddie sighed, taking a seat and dropping his bookbag on another. "That will really do me a lot of good."

✿   ✿   ✿

31

"How do you do that?" Steve asked Freddie, his eyes wide with admiration. Freddie had just finished a 360° turn complete with grab.

"I don't know," Freddie said. "I just do it."

"I could never do that," Steve said.

"Sure you could, dude," Freddie assured him. "Let me see you try it. Come on."

"Nah, I'd be too scared," Steve said. "I mean, what if I lost control and landed on my head or something?"

"You won't lose control," Freddie insisted. "Not unless you freeze up. Don't you see, Steve — it's the fear that makes you lose control."

"Great," Steve said disconsolately. "How'm I sup-posed to get rid of that?"

Freddie thought for a minute. "Maybe if you just go all the way with the move, and don't do it halfway. Try it, Steve. Just try it once, for me."

"Well . . . okay," Steve said. He started up the hill to the top of the halfpipe. "Just go all the way with it, huh?"

"That's it . . . think like you're a famous acrobat getting shot out of a cannon, or like you're a cham-pion high-diver. Stretch out your body. Yank it left, and from the waist, not the shoulders. That's where Dondi always messes up. He moves from the shoulders and winds up pulling himself right into the snow."

"Hmmm," Steve grunted, strapping on his board and adjusting his helmet. "Better get ready to call 911 just in case," he said with a bit of a grin. Then he shoved off.

Freddie watched as he slid down the slope, picking up speed. "Don't anticipate!" Freddie yelled after him. "Time it out! Keep your center of gravity low!" As Steve neared the top of the wall, Freddie unconsciously bent into a crouch, willing Steve to time the jumpoff and twist just right.

Steve, understandably a little anxious, pulled up early and didn't get the height on his jump that he needed. But he did pull well from the waist and got all the way around on his turn just before he hit the snow again. The surprise of making the move threw him off, though. After a lot of wobbling, he toppled and slid down the rest of the way on his backside.

Freddie boarded down after him, stopping just as Steve was getting up off the ground.

"I did it, kind of!" Steve said, sporting a big grin.

"I see what you mean about twisting from the waist."

"Yeah," Freddie said, nodding happily. "Next time, just don't anticipate the takeoff, and you'll nail the landing too. See, I told you you could do it."

Steve laughed. "Not like you," he said. "Oh, and that reminds me. About Clarissa?"

"Ugh," Freddie said. "Don't depress me. She's at the mall with Dondi right about now. I hope he spills ice cream right on his lap."

Steve chuckled. "That would be pretty cool," he said. "Anyway, I had an idea. Remember what I said about you being better than Dondi at snowboarding?"

"Yeah. So?" Freddie asked. "I told you already, it doesn't make any difference."

"Well, it could," Steve said. "If she could see how much better a boarder you are than Dondi, she might change her mind about who she likes best."

"Right," Freddie said hopelessly. "Anyway, I'm not that much better than him."

"Sure you are!" Steve assured him. "And since he's working all the time now, you'll be getting more practice than him, and you'll only get better! In fact,

I was thinking you could challenge Dondi to a contest and make sure Clarissa's there to see it."

"Too obvious," Freddie pointed out. Then he blinked as an idea came to him. "Unless maybe we made it a big contest, with other boarders."

"Yeah!" Steve said excitedly. "Let's do it!"

"You know, Steve," Freddie said with a smile, putting an arm around his friend's shoulders, "you're not as dumb as you look. That is a most excellent idea. Not bad at all."

The first thing the two boys needed to do was lay out their plan for Eric. It was one thing to have a big idea. But if you really wanted to think something through, Eric Schwartz was the man to see. The very next day at lunch, Freddie and Steve took him over to a table in the far corner of the cafeteria.

"So, what's up?" Eric asked when they were out of earshot of everyone else.

Freddie jumped right in. "We've got this idea for a snowboarding contest," he said. And he laid out the plan for Eric.

"Let me get this straight," said Eric when Freddie was done. "Freddie likes Clarissa, who likes Dondi. Freddie thinks that by beating Dondi in a snow-boarding contest, Clarissa will suddenly like him better than big brother?"

Freddie blinked. When Eric put it like that, it didn't sound quite as good.

Eric shook his head. "Won't it seem a little obvious to Dondi? I can't see him jumping at the chance to be made a complete fool of."

Freddie opened his mouth, but Eric wasn't finished. "And what if you don't win?" he pointed out. "Doesn't that sort of defeat the purpose?"

"He's going to win," Steve argued. "We'll only invite boarders he can beat but who can beat Dondi."

Eric looked at them both. "And no one realizes it's all a setup. Have I got it all right?"

"Yup," Steve said.

"What do you think?" Freddie asked.

"I don't know," Eric said, frowning. "Sounds risky to me. And it might not work anyway. Your biggest problem, of course, is that Clarissa doesn't seem the type of girl to be impressed by great moves on the slopes."

"Have you got any better suggestions?" Steve asked him. "Because he can't just sit here while Dondi buys Clarissa ice cream sundaes and tells her every nasty thing he knows about Freddie, can he?"

"Hmmm. I see your point," Eric said, tapping his

37

fingers on his chair. He sighed. "Well, I can't seem to think of anything better to suggest, so I'll help."

"Thanks," Freddie said. If Eric was on board, he knew there was a good chance they'd succeed — even if Eric didn't seem one-hundred-percent convinced that the plan would work.

"So what do we do first?" Steve asked.

Eric scratched his head. "Well, we've got to line up some contestants. How many were you planning on?"

"At least six, including me and Dondi," Freddie said. "Anything less and it would look funny."

"Okay," Eric agreed. "Have you got anyone in mind? How about Nate Sherman?"

"Forget it!" Steve said. "He's way better than Freddie. He and Brad Forest are the only two kids to ever go down Devil's Ravine and come out in one piece. They can do reverse somersaults on the half-pipe. Are you kidding me?"

"Hmmm. Okay, so Nate and Brad are out," Eric said, nodding. "Why don't we get a bunch of seventh- and even sixth-graders? That way, Dondi will look even worse when he loses."

"Cool!" Steve said. "How about Les Buckman?

And me, of course. I can beat Dondi, if Freddie helps me practice some more."

"That only leaves two more slots," Eric said. "Ooh, I've got it! How about Cheryl Abercrombie and Veronica McBride? They're both pretty good. And can't you just see Dondi's face when a couple of girls beat him?"

Freddie had to smile. It would bother Dondi, he knew. Dondi was one of those kids who thought boys can do any sport better than girls. "So that's six!" he said. "Great. Who's going to invite them?"

"I'll take care of it," Eric said. "That way, it'll look less like it's your idea. Once we've got everyone else lined up, you can invite Dondi."

"Who's going to be the judge?" Steve asked.

"I can do that, too," Eric said. "And I'll be emcee as well. You guys just take care of boarding, okay? Leave the rest to me."

Freddie waited until after dinner to approach Dondi about the contest. Esteban had heated up canned vegetables and prepared two boxes of macaroni and cheese. Neither of the boys complained. It was better than their dad's hopeless attempts at real cooking.

After dinner Freddie did his homework and watched his favorite show on TV. Just before bed-time he headed up to Dondi's room. The door was open, and Dondi was inside counting up his money. There seemed to be a lot of it, Freddie noticed.

"Where'd you get all that money?" he asked Dondi.

"Did I say you could come in?" Dondi responded.

"The door was open." Freddie didn't move.

"You messed up my count," Dondi complained. "Now I have to start over."

"You didn't answer me," Freddie pointed out. "Did you get paid all that money at work?"

"No, man," Dondi said with a laugh. "What do you think, the boss is gonna pay me before I even work a week? You are so dumb sometimes."

"Shut up, you jerk," Freddie shot back, his anger rising to the surface so fast that he couldn't stop it. "Why do you always call me names?"

"I didn't call you a name," Dondi said. "You called me a name. All I said was that sometimes you're dumb. And you are."

"So are you," Freddie said. "Do I get to call you 'stupid idiot'?"

"Okay, okay, get over it," Dondi said, shaking his head and rolling his eyes. "To answer your question, this is all left over from my birthday and Christmas, plus shoveling snow and stuff. I've been saving up."

"What for?" Freddie asked.

Dondi's face grew secretive, and a satisfied smile crept over it. "Something good."

"That's a lot of money," Freddie said. "You want to bet it you can beat me in a snowboarding contest?"

"Sure, right," Dondi scoffed. "And what are you going to bet? Air? I don't see your wad of cash, big guy."

Freddie steamed, but he knew he had Dondi's attention now. The offer of a bet had been a sudden inspiration, but it didn't really matter. The important thing was the contest — and Clarissa.

"You're afraid I could beat you," Freddie said. "You know I can. I always do."

"A few stupid games of Pig. And if I remember correctly, we never finished the last game," Dondi reminded him. "Besides, I go easy on you because you're smaller."

"Yeah, right," Freddie said. "I can beat you any-time I want."

"Cannot."

"Oh, yeah?" Freddie said, pouncing. "There's a contest a week from Saturday. I'm in it. Are you?"

"What contest?" Dondi asked, suddenly alert and suspicious. "I never heard about any contest."

"That's because it just got announced."

"When?"

"Today."

Dondi looked searchingly at him. "You made it up yourself," he said, seeing right through Freddie.

"No, I didn't," Freddie insisted, ready for this. "Steve Myers set it up."

"Myers? That dweeb? Ha!"

"He is not a dweeb," Freddie said. "He's a better boarder than you."

Dondi guffawed. "That kid can't board for beans. Everybody knows it."

"They only think it because you told them," Fred-die said sharply. "Are you in or not? If you're too chicken then the whole school is going to know about it. And I won't even have to tell them. There are plenty of other contestants."

"Yeah? Who?"

Freddie reeled off a few of the names.

"What about Forest and Sherman?"

"Uh, no . . . they couldn't make it." Freddie didn't volunteer that he and his friends had decided not to invite the pair.

"I don't know why *I* should, then," Dondi said. "Sounds like a contest for sixth- and seventh-grade dweebs only."

"You are chicken," Freddie taunted. "You're afraid you'll come in dead last. I see it in your eyes, you wimp."

"I'll bust your nose if you don't quit it," Dondi threatened.

"You don't want people to see me beat you," Freddie continued. "You're afraid I'll make you look bad."

Suddenly, a grin spread across Dondi's face — a confident grin that made Freddie nervous. "We'll see about that," he said. "I've got some new tricks up my sleeve."

Freddie blinked, taken by surprise by Dondi's sudden eagerness to be in the contest. Was Dondi just bluffing? Or did he really have some reason for his swagger?

"So, you want to be in the contest?" Freddie said. "Okay, you're in."

"You bet I am, squirt," Dondi said, shaking Freddie's hand extra hard. "And I'm in it to win it."

Freddie pulled his hand away. "Okay. So now you can tell me. What's the big secret, huh?"

"You'll find out soon enough," Dondi said, enjoying himself greatly. "Ooh, you're so curious! You're just dying to know. Get down and beg, and maybe I'll tell you." He gave Freddie a smug smile. "I almost told Clarissa over ice cream the other day."

That did it. Freddie roared and launched himself at Dondi. Caught off guard, the bigger boy landed with a thud on the bed. Immediately, the two brothers began pummeling each other, screaming insults at the top of their lungs.

Only their father's shouts, and his strong arms prying them apart, got through to Freddie and Dondi. Esteban shoved Freddie backward while holding Dondi off with his other hand. "Boys!" he barked commandingly. "Stop it right now!"

There was a long silence. Freddie caught his breath and waited for the pounding of his heart to slow down.

Esteban's jaw was tense, and his eyes gleamed like black coals. "You know, boys," he said in a half whisper, "how do you think your mother would feel if she came home to see somebody with a bloody nose?"

Dondi and Freddie glanced at each other then looked down at the floor guiltily.

Esteban continued, launching into his now familiar lecture about good sportsmanship. "When I was your age," he began, "I used to think winning was everything, that I always had to be better than everybody else. You have to learn to lose sometimes in life, as well as to win.

"You know," he continued, "one time I set a trap for this guy on roller skates. I knew a certain street was rough to skate, with potholes and all. But I also knew the righthand side of it was smoother than the left. So I challenged this kid to a race, and I made sure I skated on the right side. Can you guess what happened?"

Neither boy spoke.

"He fell halfway through the race, and I won," Esteban finished. "Then I turned around and saw he was bleeding very bad. A big gash in his knee." Esteban slashed a finger across his own kneecap. "He never skated again, at least not when I was around. I've felt bad from that day to this about it. That's how I learned why sportsmanship is so important." He looked at his two sons. "You boys have got to try harder to be good brothers. This fighting has got to stop. You're on the same team, amigos. Understand?"

"Yes, Papi," the boys said simultaneously.

"Okay, now go to bed. School tomorrow."

"When is Mami getting home?" Dondi asked softly.

"Soon. She had a late meeting tonight," Esteban said.

"Send her up to say good night to me, okay?" Dondi said. "I want to talk to her."

"Okay," Esteban said. "Come on, Freddie. Let's get you to bed too."

Freddie went quietly. Something had reached him in what his dad had said about the skating race. It was sort of the same, the way he was setting up this contest just so Dondi would lose. Now he felt terrible about it. He wanted to call the whole thing off. He wished Dondi had just said no.

But Dondi had said yes, and now it was too late to

back out. If he did, Freddie was the one who would look like a chicken. It would be like admitting that Dondi was better than him at everything. Bigger, faster, better-looking, funnier, cooler. Freddie sighed. No, there was no going back, he realized. The contest had to go on.

That Saturday afternoon, Freddie sat with Steve and Eric in the food court at the mall. Freddie and Steve were chowing down on Megaburgers and Megasized Maniac Fries and slurping chocolate shakes. Eric was eating his usual lunch of salad and soup, topped off with a piece of fruit.

"I don't get much exercise," he reminded people whenever they remarked about his healthy eating habits. "I've got to keep up a good diet. I like this stuff, anyway," he'd add with a smile and a shrug before digging into his greens.

Rabbit food, Freddie thought as he watched Eric eat. Poor guy. Of course, it was also true that Eric never missed a day of school and always had more energy than anybody, in spite of his disability. Freddie screwed up his face. One of these days, he

48

thought, wiping ketchup off his chin, I've gotta try that rabbit stuff.

In between bites, Eric told them about all the preparations he'd made for the big contest, which was now exactly one week away. "The article is coming out on Wednesday in the local paper and on Friday in the school news. We should have an excellent crowd. I made sure of that by announcing that all proceeds would go to charity."

"Good idea!" Steve said, then realized something. "You mean you're going to charge?" he asked.

"Why not?" Eric said with a shrug. "It's all for a good cause, and it'll bring in the crowds even better than a free ticket. If it's free, they think it can't be that good," he explained.

Freddie shook his head in admiration. "Man, you think of everything," he said.

"I try, I try," Eric said humbly, accepting the compliment.

"I've been practicing," Steve said. "I can almost do a three-sixty complete with nose grab!"

Freddie said, "I want to see Dondi's face when you bring it off!"

"About Dondi," Eric interrupted. "Is he still in?"

49

"Yeah," Freddie said. "He's all gung ho and every-thing."

"I don't get that," Steve said. "Doesn't he realize what's going to happen?"

"Apparently not," Eric said.

Freddie squirmed. Dondi did have something up his sleeve, he could tell. Dondi wouldn't have agreed to enter a contest in public if he didn't think he could win.

Suddenly he was feeling tense and anxious about the contest. With the articles in the paper, there could be a big crowd. What if he didn't win? What if something happened — if he fell, and Dondi had his best day ever? It could happen, Freddie knew. On any given day, anything could go down.

Eric interrupted his thoughts. "Say, where are we going?" he asked, wadding up his napkins and crushing his empty drink container.

"I don't know," Freddie said, looking around now. "There's Buddy's. Wanna go spy on Dondi?"

"Sure!" Steve said happily.

Freddie didn't tell them why he really wanted to spy on his brother. It had occurred to him that

Clarissa might be there too. He hoped not, but he had to take a look and make sure.

Clarissa wasn't there, Freddie quickly noted with relief. But what he did see made his worry level rise to new heights.

Dondi was in the store window, lifting a glittering new snowboard off its stand. Looking at it lovingly, he tucked it under his arm and patted it with a satisfied look, as if to say, Come to Papa!

Freddie gulped. Was this the surprise Dondi had up his sleeve?

"Hey, Freddie!" Dondi greeted him, hopping down from the display window onto the floor of the store. "That's nice, you came to visit me, man. Hey, guys." He waved to Eric and Steve.

"Hey." They waved back without enthusiasm.

"You like this board, squirt?" Dondi asked, holding it out to Freddie. "'Cause if you like it, it's yours."

Freddie stared at his brother, open-mouthed.

"Nah, just kidding. Actually, this baby's for me," Dondi said laughing as he yanked the board back.

Freddie's eyes were glued to the price tag. It was

more than three hundred dollars! "You're b-buying that?" he spluttered.

"That's right," Dondi said, looking mighty pleased with himself. "Me, myself, and I. Can't be entering contests with my ratty old board, can I?"

Dondi's old board wasn't exactly prime, Freddie had to admit, but his own was even worse. Splinters stuck out from the edges, and the layers of laminated wood were starting to come apart where the glue was wearing out.

This new board might not make Dondi a world-class snowboarder. But it could give him enough of an edge to beat Freddie and make a monkey out of him next Saturday.

Freddie swallowed hard, and Dondi laughed with pleasure. "Glad you like it, bro," he said, holding it up for Steve and Eric to admire. "Nice, huh? Maybe someday I'll let you try it out — after I break it in, of course. Like after the contest, sucker!"

With a big laugh, he headed for the checkout counter where he stowed the board behind the cash register. "Don't want anyone else buying it before I do," he explained.

"How can you afford that much?" Freddie demanded. "I saw how much birthday money you had — it's not nearly enough. And don't tell me one week's salary is going to make the difference."

"No, that's true," Dondi agreed. "But the boss likes me, see — he likes my style, the way I am with the customers and all. He told me I could put a down payment on it Friday with my first paycheck and work off the rest as I go, a little bit every week."

"Man!" Freddie said unhappily, kicking the side of the counter. "It's not fair."

"Hey, you don't like it, you can go get your own job," Dondi suggested.

"You know I'm not old enough," Freddie said through gritted teeth.

"Oh, yeah, that's right!" Dondi said, slapping his forehead as if he'd completely forgotten. "Well, be patient, squirt. Someday you can be just like me."

"I'd rather eat raw onions for a week," Freddie said, turning away. "Come on, you guys. Let's get out of here." And with Steve and Eric trailing behind, he left the store, Dondi's laughter ringing in his ears.

On Sunday afternoon, Freddie and Dondi got a ride from their dad out to the halfpipe. While Freddie was glum and silent in the backseat, Dondi, riding up front, was in rare high spirits. He bounced up and down in his seat to the beat of the music on the radio.

"Oh, yeah, oh, yeah!" he crooned tunelessly. "I can't wait to get out there with my Fantom Fish!"

He meant his snowboard, which had those words emblazoned on it in glittery neon orange. He cradled the board on his lap, beating time on it with his palms.

Freddie wished he'd be quiet for one second. It was so annoying to have to listen to Dondi when he was being a motormouth.

Freddie looked down at his own miserable snowboard. His parents had found it at a garage sale for ten dollars. It was okay for some five-year-old who was just starting out. For Freddie, even though he and the board had been through a lot together, enough was enough.

His glance kept straying to Dondi's Fantom Fish. Freddie would have given anything to have a new board like that. He knew he could be so much better with a prime piece of equipment.

That was what worried him most — that the new

board would improve Dondi's performance. How could it not?

And sure enough, it did. By his third run on the new board, Dondi was comfortable enough to try a 360° shifty, the move Freddie had always taunted him with. Dondi made it with ease. Freddie suddenly felt sick as he saw what a nightmare the contest could become.

He himself was having a really bad day on the board. He wiped out on an easy grab move then slipped and fell on his backside while just coasting downhill.

All this was making Dondi feel great, of course. And when Dondi felt great, he let everyone know about it. "Man, I am da bomb on this thing!" he shouted after completing another run.

Freddie didn't argue with him. His own confidence had been shaken, and it was showing with every run he took. "I've got to get a new board," he muttered under his breath.

But where was he going to get one? New boards cost hundreds of dollars, as Freddie well knew.

Hey, maybe I could borrow a board!

He was in midrun when the thought hit him, and

he pulled out of a move early. He lost his concentration and fell hard, sliding for about fifty feet before he could get up again.

"Boy, you're really messing up today," Dondi said with a chuckle when Freddie reached the bottom.

Freddie barely heard him. He was already going over everyone he knew, trying to figure out where he could borrow a snowboard for next Saturday. There was only one problem — everyone he knew who owned a good enough board was already in the contest!

Everyone, that was, except for two people, the two people he'd deliberately not invited — Nate Sherman and Brad Forest.

Freddie knew where to find them. They would be at the advanced slope — the one called the Vortex.

"I'll be back in a little while," he told Dondi. "I've got to go find somebody."

He was afraid Dondi would ask where he was going, or even want to come with him. But he needn't have worried. Dondi was too busy waxing his new board to care what Freddie did. Freddie pushed off, heading toward the ski lifts.

7

"Don't even touch my board, okay, man?" Nate Sherman, six feet tall, all muscle, and almost fifteen years old, looked menacingly down at Freddie. "I mean, don't even think about my board."

"Like we're really going to do you a favor after you froze us out of your contest," Brad Forest added. Brad had more freckles than anyone Freddie had ever seen, and he always looked like he'd just tasted something bad. Maybe Brad sucked on lemons for breakfast and that was why he looked like that, Freddie thought.

"Actually, I was going to invite you," Freddie lied. "But I didn't think you liked the halfpipe. I mean, you guys are always up here, doing slalom racing."

"We could show you stuff on the halfpipe," Nate

assured him. "Quit lying. You just didn't want us blowing away the competition."

"What do you think we are — stupid?" Brad added. "Use your own board."

"And what a beauty it is!" Nate chimed in. "Just look at all these nifty features!" He grabbed the board out of Freddie's hands and tossed it to Brad. "Note the shredded look around the edges. Very retro."

Brad pretended to admire it. "Smooth contours, Nate," he said, in a fake TV announcer voice. "Wish I had one just like it, don't you?"

"Ooh, can I borrow your crummy old board, Freddie? Please, please, please?" Nate taunted.

Freddie tried to grab his board but they kept pulling it away, handing it back and forth, keeping it out of his reach. "Give it back!" Freddie demanded.

"Say please," Brad demanded.

"Please," Freddie said through gritted teeth.

"Ooh, I'm scared of him," Nate said. "We'd better give big, bad Freddie his board."

"Okay, Nate," Brad said, handing it back to Freddie. "Please don't hurt us, sir," he begged piteously.

Then both he and Nate cracked up, slapping each other five as Freddie grabbed his board back and began to trudge away, the board tucked securely under his arm.

"Hey, wait a second," Nate called after him. "Where're you going, son? I've got an idea."

Freddie turned and looked at him but didn't say anything.

"I'll tell you what, Freddie, old pal," Nate went on. "I'll lend you my board for the contest, on three conditions."

"What?" Freddie asked, sure that this was just another twist of the knife.

"One: You take good care of it." Nate smiled at Brad and winked. "Two: You give it back after."

"Yeah? And three?" Freddie was half excited now. The first two conditions hadn't been too bad.

"Three: First, you have to come with us down Devil's Ravine."

"Yeah!" Brad agreed, giving Nate a slamming high-five.

"Thanks, but no thanks," Freddie said. "I'm not ready to die just yet."

"Ha! The chicken unmasked!" Nate crowed. He tucked his hands into his armpits and flapped his arms, making chicken noises at Freddie.

Freddie paid no attention. He turned and started back toward the halfpipe. He had heard plenty about Devil's Ravine, although he'd never been there. It was about a ten-minute walk from here, in an isolated part of the state forest that abutted the Snowshoe ski resort.

Devil's Ravine had a bad reputation. It had been responsible for three broken wrists, two broken legs, and one really bad injury — a boy who had spent six months in a coma before finally coming out of it. Freddie was not eager to join the list of casualties, even it not taking the dare meant he'd lose the contest.

Well, that didn't work, he told himself matter-of-factly. Now what do I do? He sat down on a snowbank to think.

He couldn't come up with anyone else to borrow a board from. He wasn't about to steal one.

"Beg, borrow, or steal," Freddie breathed, remembering the words to an old song he'd heard. "I guess begging is the only thing left."

Now that he thought of it, his birthday was only six weeks away. He was going to be thirteen. Maybe, just maybe, he could talk his parents into getting him his present early.

It wasn't likely to happen, but at least it was a plan.

Freddie decided to ask his mother instead of his father.

"Mami," he said, sitting down on the couch next to her that night and snuggling close the way he used to do when he was little. It still felt just as good to be nestled in her arms.

"What is it, baby?" she asked in a soft voice, kissing him on the forehead.

"Do we have enough money?" Freddie wondered.

"Yes, sure we do . . . if we don't overspend, we'll be fine. Why, are you worried about it?"

"Well, you see, it's just that . . . well, my birthday's coming up, and I wasn't sure you were going to be able to get me anything."

"Of course we're going to get you something!" his mother said with a laugh. "Are you kidding me?"

"I mean something good. Like a new snowboard or something."

"Is that what you want for your birthday?" his mother asked.

"Uh-huh. But a new one, you know? Not from a garage sale."

His mother sighed. "Mmmm, how much would that cost, about?" she asked.

"I don't know," Freddie lied. Then he slipped it in. "A few hundred, maybe."

"Wh—!"

"But you wouldn't have to give me a party or anything else at all, so you could use all that money to buy it for me!" Freddie threw in hurriedly.

His mother relaxed a little. "Well, maybe we could swing it," she said. "After all, it's not till March."

"But I need it right away," Freddie blurted out. "March will be too late!"

"Freddie," his mother said, holding him at arm's length so she could look him in the eye, "is that what this is all about? If you think I'm going to —"

"Winter is practically over by my birthday!" Freddie pointed out. "I wouldn't be able to use it till *next winter* if you wait!"

Again, his mother stopped to consider his words. "I see your point," she said, nodding. "I'll tell you what. I have to think about this. Let me talk to Papi, and we'll let you know, okay?"

Freddie smiled and hugged her tight. "Thank you, Mami," he said. "You're the best."

"I didn't say you were getting it," she cautioned him.

"I know," said Freddie. "You're the best anyway."

When Freddie's mom said "We'll let you know," it only ever meant one thing. So Freddie wasn't worried. In fact, he couldn't help telling Steve and Eric about the new board he was going to get and what a big difference it was going to make next Saturday.

Steve was excited. "Man, I wondered when you were going to get rid of that old board," he said.

"Hey," Eric broke in. "He does pretty well on that old board," he reminded Steve.

"Yeah, but you don't realize what a difference your board makes," Freddie told Eric. Then he wished he hadn't said it. The look on Eric's face was only there for an instant, but Freddie knew what it meant. Of course Eric didn't realize. He'd never been on a snowboard; never would be.

"I'll take your word for it" was all his friend said.

Fortunately, the bell for first period sounded at that moment. "Well, I gotta go. See you guys in English." He wheeled himself away. Steve and Freddie turned in the other direction and headed for history class.

"I shouldn't have said that to Eric," Freddie confessed.

"What?"

"'You don't realize what a difference your board makes.' It hurt Eric's feelings."

"Ah, you're too sensitive," Steve scoffed.

"No, I'm not," Freddie said. "I ought to watch my mouth a lot more."

Steve clapped him on the back. "You're okay," he said. "You're a whole lot better than some people. Your brother, for instance. Now let's get to history class."

"Thanks," Freddie said. But for some reason, the thought of Dondi being a worse person than him was troubling.

Freddie knew what his father would say: "You're both my boys. I love you both the same, and I know, deep inside, you're both good boys." That was Esteban. Freddie had had a whole lifetime to watch him, and he thought his dad was about the best person on

Earth. One day, he hoped he could look at things the way Esteban did.

"Here we are," Steve said, opening the door and going inside. Freddie followed him. Mrs. Ellis was not there yet, and everyone was standing around in groups, talking.

Freddie spotted Clarissa looking over some marked tests on Mrs. Ellis's desk. He went up to her.

"Hi, guess what?" he greeted her.

"What?"

"I'm getting a new snowboard." He flashed her a smile. That ought to impress her, he thought.

"So?" She stared at him as if he were from Mars.

Freddie felt himself blush. "Did you hear about the competition?"

"Dondi told me," she replied. "Sounds like it's going to be pretty cool."

"It's going to be awesome," Freddie agreed, relaxing a little and allowing himself to smile at her. "Are you going?"

"Oh, definitely," she said, smiling back. "I've never snowboarded myself, but it looks like a blast."

"Yeah, it is," Freddie said, nodding. "Especially with a brand-new board."

"Dondi's got a new board too," Clarissa said. "He showed it to me. It's awesome."

"Yeah, but mine's going to be even better," Freddie promised.

"You know," Clarissa said, giving him a piercing look, "you ought to lay off competing so much with your brother. Don't you think it's kind of immature?"

Freddie was speechless. He stood there as if struck by a lightning bolt. "I'm not — I mean, I d-don't —" he stammered.

Clarissa shook her head and sighed. "Dondi told me all about how you guys fight," she said. "I think it's stupid."

"He's the one who's always competing with me!" Freddie protested.

"Don't give me that," Clarissa said, folding her arms. "He's told me about some of the stuff you've pulled."

Freddie felt himself go red all over. He wanted to defend himself, to tell her his side. But it was no use. She'd never believe him, not as long as she believed Dondi.

"Good morning, class!" Mrs. Ellis stood at the

door. With a glance at each other, Freddie and Clarissa returned to their seats.

Freddie sat there, oblivious to what was going on around him. He felt like strangling Dondi. Thanks to his big brother, Clarissa thought he was an immature jerk!

That afternoon, Dondi and Freddie were on the halfpipe again. Freddie had decided not to strangle his brother after all. Instead, he was going to show him a thing or two about snowboarding. New board or not, Freddie was going to prove once and for all who was better.

He sat in the snow, waxing his old board with a new, superslick wax he'd bought at the Snowshoe ski shop. New boards ran a lot slicker than old ones, Freddie knew. By using this superwax, he hoped to make his board act more like a new one.

When he was ready, he strapped the board on and leaned into the slope, taking off down the hill. He zigged and zagged a little to get the feel of the board, then zipped up the wall and took the air.

Freddie could feel how much higher his increased speed had taken him. He had time for an extra 180° twist. By the third jump, he had taken on so much speed that his lifts were awe-inspiring.

"Wow, man, what did you do?" Dondi asked when Freddie reached the bottom.

"New kind of wax," Freddie explained.

"Oh, man, gimme some of that," Dondi said, reaching into Freddie's pocket.

Freddie grabbed the offending hand at the wrist and squeezed hard. "That's my wax," he said. "Get your own."

"You know I've got no money left over," Dondi explained. "Everything's going to pay off the board. Come on, I'll pay you back next month."

"Forget it," Freddie said. And then a thought hit him. He knew it was mean, kind of evil even. But the truth was, the superslick wax was great for an old, rough-edged board — with a new board, it would probably make things too slick. He was surprised Dondi didn't know that, but judging from the impatient look on his brother's face, he didn't.

Freddie had an image of Dondi slipping and

sliding all over the halfpipe. Even better, once the wax was on, it would be hard to get off. Dondi's practice might be set back a day or even two!

"Oh, okay," Freddie said, releasing Dondi's hand. "But you've got to buy me a new tin of wax next month. Deal?"

"Deal! Now gimme it!" Dondi grabbed the wax and sat down to wax his board.

Feeling slightly guilty, Freddie went back up the hill to try another run in the meantime. But he was going to get even with Dondi for turning Clarissa against him. "He guessed I liked her when he asked her out," Freddie muttered under his breath as he launched into another run.

This time, he performed a series of grab combinations. He skidded to a stop right in front of Dondi and showered him with powdery snow.

"Hey, quit that!" Dondi yelled.

"Done with my wax?" Freddie asked.

"Yeah, here you go." Dondi tossed it back.

"Why don't you try what I just did?" Freddie challenged him.

"You mean that pathetic bunch of grabs? No

problem, squirt." Dondi grabbed his board and headed up the hill to the top of the halfpipe.

Freddie stood there watching him. He was going to enjoy this.

"Here I go!" Dondi shouted and began his run. "Whoooaaa!" Immediately, he was wobbling, struggling to maintain his balance. Freddie's enjoyment turned to alarm when Dondi came up the wall at top speed and hit the air. His arms windmilled as he lost control of the jump. Moments later, he landed hard, crying out in pain as his knees buckled under him and he slid in a ball down the halfpipe.

Freddie raced over to him. "Dondi, are you okay?" he cried.

"My knee! Ow, it hurts!" Dondi moaned, grabbing his leg.

"Here, let me get the board off you," Freddie said, unbuckling the footstraps.

"Get away from me," Dondi growled. "This is all your fault — you knew this was going to happen!" He got up and limped away, testing his left knee gingerly.

"I didn't!" Freddie protested. But his voice faltered

71

slightly. It was true, what Dondi was accusing him of. And that made what Clarissa had said true, too. Freddie was so caught up in competing with his brother that he was willing to pull immature tricks on him — even if it meant his brother might get hurt.

What kind of person did that make him?

Freddie, your father and I have been talking it over . . ."

Freddie sat up straight at the dinner table, his eyes widening in anticipation. This was it. This was the big moment.

". . . and we've decided to get you your birthday present early."

"Yes! All right!" Freddie stood up, clapping his hands and whooping with joy. "I get my new snowboard!"

"What?" Dondi bolted upright, his hands supporting him as he leaned over the table toward his parents. "What do you mean, you're getting him a new snowboard? How come I had to buy my own?"

"Well, his birthday is coming up," Aida Ruiz explained, "and we thought —"

"You thought wrong!" Dondi exploded. "That little spoiled brat doesn't have to work, like I do. He spends all his free time getting me in trouble, and you buy him a new snowboard? Come on!"

"Donovan," Esteban said, putting out a calming hand, "try to understand. Winter's already half over, and —"

"I don't want to hear any of this!" Dondi shouted, slamming the table with his fist. "I work hard for my money, and you guys don't give me anything!"

"He's only twelve," Esteban pointed out.

"Thirteen in March," Freddie added.

"Shut up, squirt!" Dondi lashed out at him. "You guys wouldn't be so nice to your little angel if you knew what a brat he was."

"What are you talking about?" Freddie asked, his voice rising. "If they want to get me an early birthday present —"

"Be quiet, I said," Dondi ordered him. "Mami, Papi, he nearly got me killed today, did you know that? Ask your precious Freddie about the wax he made me use."

"I did not make you use it — you took it out of my hand!" Freddie protested.

"You took it out to tempt me!" Dondi insisted. "You knew I'd grab it. And you knew that with my new board, it would be too slick and make me fall. But you let me go right ahead. You didn't say anything."

Freddie was silent for a moment as he searched for the right response. Dondi jumped right into the void.

"You see, he can't even deny it!" he said, pointing an accusing finger. "He made me twist my knee! Look how bad it is!" He limped away from the table, wincing with each step on the injured knee.

"He's faking it!" Freddie said, his voice squeaking in his frustration.

"Oh yeah, smart guy?" Dondi said, a smile of victory coming over his face. "Then how do you explain this?" He rolled up the leg of his sweatpants to show a knee that was somewhat swollen and even a little black and blue. "So I'm faking it, huh?" He turned to his parents. "Go ahead, then, get your little angel his new snowboard. Reward him by giving him an early birthday present. What do I care? You all hate me anyway!"

With that, he threw down his napkin and stormed out of the kitchen.

"Freddie, is what Dondi says true?" his mom asked, a look of pain on her face. "Did you know the wax would make him fall?"

"Freddie, tell us the truth," his dad said softly, giving him the look that always made Freddie want to disappear into the floor.

"I didn't do it, Papi," Freddie said, pleading for understanding. "Dondi just took it out of my hand. You know how he is!"

Well, technically, it was the truth. Dondi had taken the wax right out of Freddie's hand. But it was also true that Freddie had held it out to him, had known what might happen; that he'd relished the thought of Dondi losing control of his board. And now, deep inside, he knew he was lying to his parents.

But what else was he supposed to do? If he admitted having those thoughts, they wouldn't get him his new snowboard — and Freddie had to have it in time for the big contest!

"All right, then," his mother said quietly. "If you say so, I'll believe you. You've always been an honest boy, Freddie, so we're going to trust you this time."

"Thank you, Mami," Freddie whispered, looking down at the floor. "May I be excused? I'm kind of tired, and I want to get my homework done."

"Of course," his mother said. Freddie left the room quickly, wanting to get out of there as soon as possible. He didn't really have that much homework, and he wasn't that tired. But he couldn't stand the look his father was still giving him — the look that said, I know you, Freddie Ruiz. And you're lying.

Freddie went upstairs, hoping that would be the end of it. Tomorrow maybe he'd have his new snowboard, and Saturday he'd use it to win the contest. And after that, he promised himself, after that he would make a real effort to be nicer to Dondi, no matter how bad Dondi was to him.

Late that night, after he'd turned out the light and was lying in bed, Freddie heard the door to his room open. His father stood in the doorway, hidden by the darkness. But even in the dark, Freddie could still feel his dad's eyes seeing right through him.

"Freddie," Esteban whispered. "Are you awake?"

"Mmm?" Freddie replied, feigning sleepiness.

Esteban came and stood over the bed. "I want to know something, son," he said. "I heard what you said before, and I always want to believe you. But I saw Dondi's knee, and his anger. And so I want to know this: In your heart, did you know Dondi wouldn't be able to control his board with that slick wax you let him have?"

Freddie was silent. He held his breath, listening to his heart pound. He wondered if his dad could hear it, it was so loud.

Esteban sighed deeply, sadly. "You know," he said, "all I really want in life is for my two sons to get along; to love each other like brothers should. When I was young, my brothers and I, we would have done anything for each other, we loved each other so much. I don't know what I've done wrong with you and Dondi, but it must have been very bad."

Freddie felt lower than a worm. Then his father sat down on the bed beside him and put a tender hand on Freddie's shoulder.

"Promise me something, Freddie," Esteban said. "Promise me that, no matter what's happened up to now, you'll always be a good, true brother to Dondi from now on. He may have his problems, but he's still your brother, and you've got to stick by him."

"But he hates me," Freddie managed to squeak past the lump in his throat.

"No," Esteban replied. "He may get angry with you, but underneath, he loves you, Freddie. He's the only brother you've got. So promise me — promise me you'll be a friend to him from now on, and a true brother. Promise?"

Freddie nodded. "I promise," he whispered. His father patted his head and then left the room. Freddie lay there, alone in the darkness, wishing he'd never let Dondi have that wax. More than that — he wished they'd never had a fight in their whole lives. He wished he could take back every mean thing he'd ever said to Dondi.

The feeling lasted until the following day at lunch period, when Freddie caught sight of Dondi walking with Clarissa in the lunchroom. The two of them were ahead of Freddie, who was walking with Steve and Eric. Dondi had his arm around Clarissa's shoulder. But what really made Freddie burn was the fact that Dondi wasn't limping — not one little bit!

Dondi was saying something to Clarissa, gesturing with his free hand to indicate a slip and fall. Freddie guessed immediately that was telling her about the day before and how Freddie had set him up.

Sure enough, at that very moment Clarissa turned and saw Freddie. She gave him a look of disgust, then turned away again.

Freddie could stand it no longer. "Man, I hate that Dondi!" he said to his friends. "I am going to beat him so bad on Saturday."

"What'd he do now?" Eric asked. Then he turned and saw Dondi sitting down at a table with Clarissa. "Oh. I see," he said. "Hmmm."

"Don't worry about it, Freddie," Steve consoled him. "Too bad Clarissa didn't see him fall. Man, that was such a good trick, what you did with that wax."

Freddie winced, his father's words crowding his brain. "Yeah, well, Saturday I'm going to beat him fair and square. That's gonna be the day."

Steve grinned. "With your new board, you're a lock to win!"

He slapped Freddie on the back, and Freddie nodded, trying to look confident. The only trouble was, he couldn't stop thinking about the look

Clarissa had just given him. Even if he did win, it might be just one more example of how he competed with Dondi, and it would prove to her once and for all that he was as immature as she thought he was!

10

Freddie didn't cheer up until that evening when his mother came through the door with a long, thin, gift-wrapped package. "Happy early birthday!" she said.

Esteban added his congratulations. "Use it in good health," he said. But his eyes said, Remember your promise.

Freddie took the package and tore off the wrapping. "Awesome!" he gasped. The shiny new board was black with red dragon designs. He held it up to admire it. It was even cooler looking than Dondi's — smaller, but sleeker. "Mami, Papi, thank you so much!" Freddie exclaimed. "You're the best!"

Dondi must have heard him and figured out what was going on by the joyous tone of his voice, because he now threw open the kitchen door and started yelling at the top of his lungs. "I can't believe you got it for him!" he howled. "After you saw what he did to my knee!"

"Dondi, calm down," Aida said. "We just felt that since winter is half over already —"

"That is so lame!" Dondi protested. "You have to pay for *my* board now! Otherwise it's unfair!"

"Donovan," Esteban said, "please don't spoil Freddie's happiness. This is his one and only birthday present from us. Let him enjoy it."

"Yeah, right," Dondi said. "Happy unbirthday, squirt. Enjoy your new board — not!" He left the kitchen, then came back, grabbed a big bag of potato chips, and left again.

Freddie's parents looked at each other and sighed mournfully. "I'm so sorry about Dondi, Freddie," his mom said. "He'll calm down about it after a while. I just wish he didn't have to rain on your parade."

Freddie was silent, but inside, he felt anything but sorry. Any concerns he'd felt over the contest were wiped away by Dondi's behavior. And now, thanks to his fabulous new board, the contest would be a fair one, and Freddie knew that in any fair snowboarding contest, he would win.

He stroked the edges of his new board lovingly, smiling with satisfaction. He couldn't wait till Saturday.

The next afternoon, Freddie got to know his new board on the halfpipe. From the first moment, they were made for each other. Stunts Freddie had had problems with before were now easy for him. The board felt both lighter and stronger than his old one and glided much more smoothly.

Dondi, who had been so confident on his new board when Freddie was using his old one, now seemed more tentative. Obviously, the possibility of losing was on Dondi's mind. After twenty minutes or so, he picked up his board and walked away without a word.

Freddie watched him go and thought about following him. But he figured he'd find out where Dondi had gone later. Right now, he was too busy having fun to care. If Dondi was going to give up a chance to practice, that was fine with Freddie.

But later that day, when Freddie asked Dondi where he'd been, Dondi was very secretive. "None of your business," he said. Freddie began to get suspicious, and even a little worried. Dondi surely had something up his sleeve.

On Thursday, Dondi went to work, and Freddie practiced with Steve. "You're gonna wipe the floor with him, Freddie," Steve assured him.

Freddie grinned. He had already improved more in two days on his new board than he had all winter on his old one. He was ready for the competition.

So on Friday morning, when Dondi came up to him in the living room, Freddie was totally unprepared for his brother's announcement.

"I'm quitting the competition," Dondi said.

Freddie was stunned. "What? What do you mean, you're quitting?"

"Yeah, I'm out. Forget it." Dondi was looking him right in the eye, a little grin creasing the corner of his mouth.

"What are you talking about? I don't get it!" Freddie said.

"What part of 'out' don't you understand?" Dondi

asked. "You go ahead and compete. I don't need that kid stuff."

"Oh, I get it," Freddie said. "You're afraid I'm gonna beat you. That's it, isn't it?"

"No way, man," Dondi said. "I just decided it's immature to keep competing with you."

Freddie reddened, sure that Dondi had used the word *immature* on purpose to remind him of Clarissa. "Cop-out!" he said. "You're chicken, and you know it!"

Dondi's eyes grew menacing. "You're lucky Papi's around, squirt, or I'd make you pay for that."

"Step outside and make me pay," Freddie challenged him.

"No, I don't think so," Dondi said with an above-it-all air. "Mami and Papi wouldn't approve of my beating you up."

"Chicken."

"And it's not that at all, Freddie. Really."

"Oh, sure it isn't. I believe that."

"Actually, I've decided the halfpipe is played out. I'm getting into downhill."

"Downhill?" And then Freddie knew where Dondi had gone that afternoon when he'd walked away from the halfpipe. "This is all about Brad and Nate, isn't it?" he asked.

"Yeah, as a matter of fact," Dondi admitted.

"I knew it!" Freddie said. "They're always saying how lame the halfpipe is and how it's no challenge for them anymore."

"For me either," Dondi said, thrusting his chin out defiantly. "You want to race me on the downhill, fine. I'm up for it anytime you are. Forget the half-pipe."

Freddie shook his head in dismay. Dondi had completely turned the tables on him. All his plans for the competition, and now Dondi was pulling out, just like that. "You stupid lame jerk!" Freddie cried. "You're chickening out and you know it!"

"Okay, that's it!" Dondi said, raising his fists.

Freddie leaped at him, sending him reeling backward. The two boys collapsed onto the sofa, their fists flying at each other. Freddie took a shot to the eye, then in a fury started flailing for all he was worth.

Suddenly, he was yanked away by strong hands. "Dondi!" his father shouted. "Stop this right now. Go wait for the school bus!"

"Yes, Papi," Dondi said, dusting himself off and grabbing his book bag. "But he star—"

"I don't want to hear about it!" Esteban said firmly in a tone Freddie hadn't heard from him in months. "Leave the house, now!"

Dondi clucked his tongue. "You always think it's my fault," he grumbled as he went outside, slamming the front door behind him.

Esteban turned to Freddie. "And you!" he said, his jaw tight. "What did you promise me? What?"

Freddie looked down at the floor. He wished he could just disappear right then and there. He'd promised his dad he'd be a good brother to Dondi, and he'd broken his word.

"I'm sorry, Papi," he said. "It won't happen again."

His dad looked closely into his face and sighed. "You look like you're going to get a shiner on that eye. Go put an ice pack on it."

Freddie winced. He could already feel the eye swelling up. "Great," he said. "I'm going to be late for school, too."

"I'll drive you," Esteban said. "First, clean yourself up."

Freddie went to the kitchen and took out the ice pack that was always there for an emergency. A black eye, a competition without a rival, and now Papi was disappointed in him again. What a great way to start the day.

Freddie had left the competition in the capable hands of Eric Schwartz, and Eric did not disappoint. On Saturday afternoon, the halfpipe was crowded with onlookers: kids from the middle school, mostly, some with their parents or brothers and sisters. There had to be at least a hundred people, Freddie estimated.

He looked around for Clarissa but didn't see her in the crowd.

She was probably watching Dondi on the downhill slopes, Freddie knew. He felt like crying. All these other people were going to see him do his thing on his new board, and he barely even cared. Why bother, if she wasn't there?

Esteban and Aida weren't, either. Neither Freddie nor Dondi had wanted them around to see this

90

competition. Dondi hadn't wanted them to see him lose, Freddie figured. And as for Freddie himself, he didn't want them catching on to the fact that he'd set Dondi up.

Oh, well, it didn't matter now. In fact, now that Dondi wasn't here, he wished he'd invited his parents. At least they would have seen how good he was and known the money they'd spent on his new board hadn't been wasted.

Freddie said hello to Eric, Steve, the other competitors, and lots of other people he knew. Eric was seated behind a long table, where he would be judging the boarders on the quality of their moves. Over his head was a banner that read CRESTVIEW MIDDLE SCHOOL SNOWBOARDING CONTEST.

Sighing, Freddie headed up to the top of the half-pipe.

A few minutes later, there was a loud squawk as Eric turned on the megaphone he'd borrowed for the day. His voice reverberated out over the white landscape, echoing off the slopes. "Good afternoon, everyone," he said. "And welcome to the first-ever Crestview Middle School snowboarding contest!" Freddie saw the crowd applauding, but he couldn't hear anything except whistling and hooting. The gloves people were wearing muffled the clapping.

"I'm your host, Eric Schwartz, thank you very much." Another wild burst of whistles and whoops. "Thank you. As I was saying before I was so rudely interrupted, today's contestants are . . ."

He went on to name them. Freddie looked around at the small knot of kids, each wearing a number on his or her back. Freddie was number 1, reflecting his precontest rating. Eric had made up those ratings himself. As the top-ranked boarder, Freddie would get to go last.

He wished the other boarders good luck, as his father had taught him to do. "It doesn't jinx you to wish other people the best," he would say. "It means you hope they do their best and you do your best, and let the best one win. You understand, Freddie?"

He hadn't then, but now Freddie thought he was starting to get the bigger picture. He certainly felt that way today. "Good luck, Veronica, Paul, Les," he said, slapping five with each of them. "Cheryl . . . Hey, Steve." He gave Steve a big bear hug.

"Dondi's a creep for not being here," Steve said in Freddie's ear.

"Yeah, well, what are you gonna do?" Freddie replied with a shrug. "Go out there and do like I showed you, man."

Steve gave him a thumbs-up. He was wearing the number 4 on his back, but that was only because Eric had been charitable. Steve hadn't wanted to go first — or to wear number 6, for that matter. It would have been embarrassing. None of the other contestants had complained, even if they whispered about it in private.

Les Buckman went first. As he went through his first run — each contestant would get two runs — Eric called out each move as it was made. "Method . . . stalefish . . . lien air," he announced as Les did a series of grabs. Les completed them all and landed okay, but there was nothing inspiring about the performance, Freddie noticed. The applause was polite, except for Les's family and best friends, who whooped it up as best they could.

Next was Cheryl Abercrombie. She was pretty good, Freddie knew. She got a lot of air on her stunts, but she also fell a lot. That's what happened this time, on her fifth and final move — a full 360° turn. She spun out at the bottom and lay on the ground for a few moments before slowly getting up and unstrapping her board.

After each run, Eric would announce the boarder's score. There were individual scores for each move and an overall score for the run on a scale of 0 to 10. Les had scored a 7.0 for his overall — Eric was obviously feeling generous today, Freddie thought — and Cheryl had scored a 6.5. She surely would have beaten Les if she hadn't fallen. Now she'd have to step it up and try harder stuff just to catch up.

Steve was next. Freddie watched with his fingers crossed as Steve headed down the halfpipe. Steve looked nervous heading into his first move. But once he got into the air, he led with his waist, just as Freddie had taught him, and landed a 360° turn. It was the hardest move in Steve's bag of tricks, and he'd done it perfectly!

Now he moved with more confidence, more relaxation. "Shifty," Eric announced as Steve wiggled his board from side to side in midair. "Method . . . method . . . and a stalefish," he said as Steve twisted right, reaching around with his left hand to grab the left rear side of the board. He landed with a wobble and then skidded into the fence that protected the spectators. "Let's give him a hand for that outstanding performance!" Eric said. "Steve Myers — that's an 8.5, a 7.0, and a 6.0, with an overall score of 7.25!"

Steve pumped his arms in the air. For one brief shining moment, at least, he was in first place — the king of the world. Freddie grinned, feeling great for Steve. "That's my boy!" he shouted, applauding and whistling. "Go, Steve!"

It was Veronica McBride's turn now. Veronica had always been an outstanding athlete. She was on Freddie's baseball team, and she was the best first baseman in the league. She was tied for third in home runs and first in stolen bases. All-star all the way. She was not a bad snowboarder either, and she'd been at it for only two years.

"Nose grab . . . tail grab . . . lien air . . ." Eric's voice echoed up to Freddie. "And a full three-sixty!"

"Man, she's good," said Paul Pierog, the number-two ranked boarder whom they'd invited to join the contest when Dondi quit. Paul was an eighth-grader and had to be at least six feet tall. He played center for the basketball team and was also captain of the chess team. Sort of an athletic brainiac, Freddie mused. A nice kid, too, and he did some beautiful moves. A sky-high 360°, a combo method/shifty, and a nose grab/tail grab, among others. He ended with an overall 8.75. Pretty good.

Paul's run would have made anything Dondi could do look pathetic, Freddie thought, sighing. But Freddie knew he himself could beat Paul's run with even a half-decent performance.

Adrenaline shot through Freddie's system when he heard Eric call his name and number. He slid straight down the halfpipe, gathering speed for his first jump. Launching high into the air, he twisted into a full 360° turn, grabbing the nose of his board at the same time. So high had he gone that he could have done an extra half turn.

And that was exactly what he did next — an incredible 540°! He landed smoothly, hearing the roar of the crowd from below. He had lost hardly any speed, and now on the spur of the moment he decided to try something he'd never done before — two complete turns. A 720°! Why not? he reasoned.

Who cared if he fell? Clarissa wasn't there to see it. Neither was Dondi, or his parents.

Freddie crouched down a little as he approached the top of the wall and sprung into the twist just as he caught air. The ground below him spun as he turned at top speed, once around, then twice! He hit the slope hard but managed to stay on his board. Two final grab moves completed his incredible run, and he skidded to a stop, his fist pumping high over his head.

". . . for an incredible 9.5 overall, folks!" Eric was yelling.

Freddie felt the exhilaration for only a moment. Then he remembered that it was all for nothing, and his shoulders slumped.

Then he saw his parents watching him with pride plastered all over their smiling faces. He went over to them and gave them each a big hug. "How'd you know about this?" he asked.

"Some big secret," Aida said. "Your friends calling all the time, leaving messages. The article in the newspaper."

"We're so proud of you, son," his father said, hugging him.

"It's the new board," Freddie said. "Thanks again, you guys."

"We're so glad we got it for you," his mom said.

Then Eric's voice came through the megaphone again. "Time for the second and final run, everyone. Boarders, take your positions."

"I'd better get going," Freddie said.

"Good luck, son," Esteban said, waving after him.

The second run went much like the first. Freddie, who was feeling loose as a goose, added all kinds of flourishes to his second run and finished far ahead of the competition.

Afterward, when Eric presented him with the trophy, Freddie held it aloft to show the crowd. He smiled and waved his thanks as they applauded him. But inside, he felt emptier than ever. Without Dondi in the competition, it was a hollow triumph.

As he followed his parents back to the lodge, he caught sight of Dondi, talking with Nate and Brad — and Clarissa. Freddie felt the lump rise in his throat and he beat his trophy against his thigh in frustration.

"What's the matter, Freddie?" his mother asked, her brow furrowed anxiously.

"Nothing. It's nothing," Freddie muttered. "Let's just get out of here, okay?" he asked, tucking his board under his arm and trudging toward the exit, not looking behind him even once.

Dondi did not come home in the car with them. He was going to get a ride with Clarissa's parents — Dondi was taking her to the movies at the mall.

All night long, Freddie lay in bed, watching the TV but not really paying attention. His mind was on Dondi and Clarissa. Right about now, they'd be sitting in the movie theater . . . in the dark . . . and Dondi would be sneaking his arm around her shoulders. . . .

When Dondi finally got home, he was in a mood to rub it in. This day, which was supposed to be the day of Freddie's triumph, had turned into a day of absolute, total misery.

"Hey, squirt!" Dondi said, poking his head into the bedroom. "Bedtime so early?"

"Shut up," Freddie muttered.

"Excuse me? I didn't hear you," Dondi said, coming in. "Would you like to say that real loud, so Mami and Papi can hear you?"

99

"I said shut up!" Freddie said, raising his voice just enough but not too much.

"Ooh, Freddie's feeling cranky tonight," Dondi said, smiling mischievously. "Maybe I can cheer you up. Want to hear about the movie we saw? Me and Clarissa?"

"Jerk!" Freddie spat out. "I hate you!"

"Aw, shucks, brother," Dondi said. "That's not very sporting of you. And I heard you were quite the sport today. King of the halfpipe peewee league, huh? Got a big plastic trophy too, I see. Very nice." Dondi picked up the trophy and tossed it from hand to hand.

"Get your hands off it!" Freddie leapt up out of bed and yanked the trophy from Dondi's grasp.

"Touchy, touchy," Dondi said, backing up a step. "Sorry I spoiled your big day," he said. "But Papi is right, you know. Brothers shouldn't compete. It's immature."

"Oh, so you're the mature one now," Freddie said. "You don't compete. Not much. Tell me you didn't go after Clarissa just because you guessed I liked her."

"Me? Would I do a thing like that?" Dondi asked, batting his eyes innocently.

"You know you did," Freddie said.

"Well, maybe I did and maybe I didn't," Dondi said. "You'll never know, will you? But I'll tell you one thing — even if I broke up with her tomorrow, she'd never go out with you. 'Cause she knows what you're really all about."

"Get out of my room!" Freddie shouted. "Papi, Mami, he's in my room! Get him out of here before I kill him!"

"I'm going, I'm going," Dondi said. "Don't be such a sore loser, squirt. She just likes me better than you, that's all."

Before Freddie could say anything, Dondi was out the door. Freddie pulled the blankets over his head and fought back the tears. He was going to get even with Dondi, one way or another. No way was he about to let his brother get off so easily.

In fact, Freddie knew exactly what he was going to do next. He was going to take up downhill boarding. If the past was any indication, before long he'd be better than Dondi at it. And this time, Dondi wouldn't be able to run away from the competition.

On Sunday night it snowed. Boy, did it snow — eight powdery inches by Monday morning, when the sun finally came back out. "Yes!" Freddie said, looking out the window. A radio announcement confirmed that school had been canceled for the day. "I've got to go outside and do some street boarding!"

"Out of my way, dork!" Dondi said, racing past him to the coat closet. The boys jostled each other, reaching for their coats, gloves, hats, scarves, and ski boots. But the jostling was good-natured for once — the sight of all that fresh snow had banished all bad thoughts from their heads. Then it was a headlong sprint for the garage to grab their boards.

"We'll be able to shove off right out the garage door!" Dondi said gleefully. The Ruizes' driveway ran downhill, and their street dropped off to the right. There would be no cars out on the back streets for at least a few precious hours because the plows would be busy cleaning up the main roads.

"I'm going to run by Steve's house," Freddie said. Steve lived just around the corner.

"Okay, I'll follow you," Dondi said, lifting the garage door and strapping on his board.

Freddie whooshed out of the garage into the powdery snow. He and Dondi had the street totally to themselves. There was not a track or a footprint anywhere. "Whooooo!" Freddie shouted as powder flew everywhere. The wind stung his face, and the sun shone brightly off the snow. Behind him, he could hear Dondi yelling happily at the top of his lungs.

Freddie skidded to a stop in front of Steve's house, sending a sky-high shower of snow into the air. Steve must have seen him because he threw open the front door and called, "I'll be right there!"

A few minutes later, the three were boarding all over the streets of Crestview. They struggled to climb up the hills but it was well worth it coming back down.

The three boys stopped by a railing at the entrance to Ridge Park.

"Hey. Let's board the park!" Steve said, looking through the bars of the railing.

"Yeah," Dondi said, "we could go down the embankment." He pushed off through the open gate with Steve right behind him.

Freddie followed them into the park, amazed at what a good snowfall could do. It was as if the whole slate between him and Dondi had suddenly been wiped clean, as if their problems had been covered over with a fresh layer of pure, white, unspoiled snow.

All their fights were forgotten, all their grudges forgiven. They were friends again, and brothers too. Even Dondi and Steve were getting along!

Freddie should have known it was too good to last. At that very moment, he heard a familiar pair of voices calling, "Dondi! Yo, man, over here!"

Nate Sherman and Brad Forest came zooming up to the three boys. "Hey, Dondi," Nate said. "Fancy meeting you here." He looked at Freddie and Steve. "I see you brought the junior brigade."

"You babysitting today?" Brad asked him.

Dondi looked embarrassed. "I was just leading Hansel and Gretel here into the heart of the woods," he joked.

Nate and Brad laughed. "Watch out they don't have any bread crumbs to find their way home," Brad said.

Freddie stood there, taking it all in. He glanced at Steve, who seemed equally at a loss for words.

"This beats halfpipe any day," Dondi said. "I told the squirt it was better, but he didn't believe me. Did you?"

Freddie's eyes narrowed as he stared back at Dondi. "You're a total chicken, Dondi. You quit that contest because you knew I could beat you. Downhill had nothing to do with it."

"Oh, yeah?" Dondi said, strutting for his eighth-grade friends. "You want to see who's chicken?"

"Anytime!" Freddie shot back.

"Freddie," Steve said, a note of caution in his voice.

Freddie ignored him. "You want a downhill race, you've got it, punk!"

"Oh, I'm a punk? Well, you're a squirt. King of the halfpint, oh, I mean pipe." Dondi shared a mean-spirited laugh with Nate and Brad. "Okay, shorty. We'll see who's a punk. You and me, one on one — down Devil's Ravine!"

Freddie gasped. "Devil's Ravine? Are you out of your gourd?"

"Wooo-hooo!" Nate cheered. "All right! The little guy's scared now!"

"Busted! In your face, shorty!" Brad said, piling it on.

"Who's a chicken now, punk?" Dondi said, his face only inches from Freddie's.

Freddie stared back at Dondi. Why was Dondi doing this crazy thing? Just to impress those two gorillas? "Dondi . . ." he said falteringly.

"Come on, come on. Are you in or out?" Dondi demanded.

Freddie was silent, searching Dondi's eyes. Dondi wasn't as good a boarder as Freddie, and both of them knew it. If they went through with this dare, Dondi might end up in the hospital — or even worse!

He saw fear in Dondi's eyes then. Dondi didn't want to do this any more than he did. But then why had he even brought it up?

Suddenly Freddie understood. Dondi had set a clever trap for him. He had dared him to board down Devil's Ravine, sure that Freddie would say

no. When he did, Dondi would be off the hook —
he'd never have to brave the dangerous slope, and
Freddie would look like the one who was chicken.

"Dondi," Freddie said in a voice that was almost a
whisper, "it's stupid to do something so dangerous.
Neither of us is a good-enough downhill boarder yet."

"Keep those excuses coming," Dondi said. He
gave Nate and Brad a triumphant smile. "Now we
know who's afraid and who's not."

"I'm not afraid!" Freddie insisted.

"'I'm not afraid!'" Dondi mimicked him in a
frightened voice.

"Say what you want, I'm not doing it." Freddie
stood firm. "I promised Papi."

"Baby promised his papi!" Dondi said in a baby
voice. Nate and Brad howled with laughter, slapping
Dondi on the back.

"Come on, Freddie," Steve said. "Let's get out of
here. We don't need to be around these losers."

Freddie nodded and followed Steve as he pushed
off. The taunts followed them.

"You did the right thing," Steve told him when
they next stopped for a rest. "It's not worth anyone
getting hurt over."

"I hate that Dondi," Freddie replied, swallowing hard.

"Never mind him," Steve advised. "Like you said, he's a punk. My dad always says if you want to know what somebody's like, take a look at who their friends are." He grinned at Freddie and winked.

Freddie laughed at the thought of it. He had great friends — Steve, Eric, and lots of others. Dondi was stuck with Nate Sherman and Brad Forest. What good were they?

He felt sorry for Dondi, suddenly. It was kind of pathetic, the way he'd put out that dare just to impress those two jerks.

"Yeah, I guess I did do the right thing," Freddie said, shaking his head with a smile of satisfaction.

When he heard about it the next day, Eric agreed wholeheartedly. "Going down Devil's Ravine would have been a big mistake," he said in the cafeteria. "Being seriously injured is no fun. Take it from one who knows, okay?"

Freddie could only imagine what Eric went through every day of his life, ever since that day the car had hit him. No, it wouldn't have been worth it, taking that risk.

They went on to talk about other things. "The whole school knows about you winning the contest," he told Freddie. "But unfortunately, a lot of them are saying it was rigged. The best boarders hadn't taken part — Nate Sherman, Brad Forest, Dondi . . ."

"Dondi? They're saying he's one of the best boarders?" Freddie asked in surprise.

"A couple of people said that," Eric confirmed. "Hey, he hangs out with Brad and Nate, so I guess the reputation rubs off."

"Hmmm."

"Now don't go getting any ideas," Eric warned him.

"I could make it down that ravine," Freddie said coolly.

"Maybe you could," Eric said. "But it's not worth taking the chance. Anyway, your brother would wipe out for sure. He might really get hurt. You know about those other poor kids —"

"I know, I know. That's why I turned it down," Freddie said.

Just then, Clarissa walked by their table. "Hi, Eric," she said with a smile. Then the smile vanished. "Hi, Freddie." She continued on her way — right to Dondi's table, where she gave him a dazzling smile.

Freddie saw red. Everything Dondi had ever done to him crystallized in that one instant. His promise to his father flew right out of his head. His good feelings toward Dondi disappeared. His healthy fear of Devil's Ravine was gone. So everyone thought the contest had been rigged, huh? That the best boarders hadn't even competed? He'd show them!

When Dondi got up to dump his trash, Freddie grabbed his arm. "You're on," he said coldly.

"Huh?" Dondi turned to face him. "What did you say?"

"I said you're on. Devil's Ravine. You and me. *Mano a mano.*"

Dondi blinked in shock. His jaw dropped.

"What's the matter, Dondi?" Freddie said. "Not up to your own dare?"

Dondi's face hardened. He pointed a finger at Freddie and said, "You want it? You got it. Only one of us is gonna win this time, squirt."

Freddie sped down the slope, out of control and at top speed. The rock just ahead was coming straight at him, as fast as a speeding car. He tried to get an edge, to steer the board away from the half-hidden boulder. But it was impossible. He started to scream just before he slammed into it!

Freddie awoke with a start and sat bolt upright in bed. Sweat was pouring down his face, and he was gasping for breath. Had it really been only a dream?

It had seemed so real. Freddie had never been to Devil's Ravine in winter, but he'd hiked there in summer once. It was a steep drop between two hillsides with several spots that would be good jumpoff points.

But Devil's Ravine also had lots of blind turns, and

in places there were fallen trees and sharp rocks jutting up from the ground. Now, in winter, those rocks and fallen trees would be half hidden and doubly treacherous.

Freddie looked at his alarm clock. It was 4:15 A.M. He had to get back to sleep or he'd be too tired to handle his math test later in the day. He lay down again and shut his eyes. But his heart kept pounding, too fast and too loud. And the image of the rock speeding at him wouldn't fade from his mind.

He wound up rising at 5:30, unable to stand it any longer. Yawning, he got washed and dressed and went downstairs to make himself breakfast. He watched early morning cable TV as he ate and waited for Dondi.

Around 7:15, Dondi came down the stairs, toweling his long hair dry. "Hey, you're up early," he said when he saw Freddie.

"Dondi, I've got to talk to you," Freddie said.

"What? You chickening out again?" Dondi asked. Freddie thought his voice sounded just a little bit hopeful.

"Dondi, just listen for a minute. I was there once, during the summer. I saw the slope and the rocks and stuff. And I'm not sure I can make it down Devil's Ravine without getting hurt. I mean really hurt. And, well, I don't know how to say this, 'cause you're not going to like it . . . but if I can't do it, how are you going to do it?"

"What are you saying?" Dondi asked. "Are you saying you're better than me?"

"Dondi . . ."

"'Cause if that's what you're saying, you're just wrong, man. Especially in downhill. I've been practicing."

"Once, you practiced."

"Twice," Dondi corrected him. "But that's not the point. I'm good, man. You should see me going down the intermediate slope."

"This is Devil's Ravine. It's a little different."

"You are chicken," Dondi said.

"Aren't you?" Freddie said. "Or are you so stupid that you think you're Superman or something?"

"Look, you want to back out, back out. I don't care. Just say you're chicken and get it over with."

Freddie grunted in sheer frustration. Why wouldn't Dondi listen? "I'm trying to do you a favor, you idiot!" he bellowed.

113

"Don't do me any favors, okay?" Dondi said. "And don't waste my time. You have two choices — you can back out and be a chicken, or you can race me down Devil's Ravine and be a loser. Ha! Yeah! That's your choice!" He flicked his towel playfully at Freddie and turned to go.

"You're wrong, big shot," Freddie called after him, white with anger. "I've got a third choice. I can race you down Devil's Ravine and win!"

Freddie grabbed his book bag and went out the front door, slamming it behind him. As he walked down the street toward the school bus stop, he was sure he felt his father's eyes on him.

Freddie turned to see if his father really was looking through the window. But the shade was down. Esteban was still sleeping. But Freddie could see those eyes in his mind, accusing, pleading, and finally, disappointed.

Freddie trudged on toward the corner. The guilt was overpowering. But there was no way out now. The race would have to go on.

"I can't believe you're doing something so incredibly stupid!" Eric Schwartz said, clapping his hands to his head. "What is wrong with you? Have you totally, once and for all, lost your coconut?"

"I know," Freddie said miserably, cradling his chin in his hands as they sat at the lunch table. "It really bites, but trust me, it's too late. There's no way I can back out now."

"I don't believe you," Eric said, shaking his head. "There's got to be a way out. I know it's hard, but try to use your withered, pathetic brain and come up with a solution, okay?"

"Hey, I've got an idea!" Freddie said, a little too brightly. "I can lose on purpose, admit Dondi's better than me at absolutely every single thing in the entire universe, and for a bonus, I can be called a chicken by every single person I know for the rest of my miserable life! Great idea!"

"Maybe you should consider it," Eric replied, not smiling.

Freddie was caught up short. "Wait. You're not really suggesting I should do that, are you? Because, like, I thought you were my friend."

"I am your friend," Eric said softly. "Look at me. I know what happens when your body gets hit by a hard, immovable object, okay?"

Freddie looked down at the table and sat silently for a long moment. "I'm sorry, Eric," he said. "I know you're trying to help. But believe me, it's too far gone. There is no help. I'm just going to have to do this and hope I make it in one piece."

He looked up and saw Clarissa standing by the stairway door. She was waving at him, motioning for him to come over. "Excuse me a minute," he told Eric. "I've got to go talk to somebody."

Eric wheeled himself around so he could see who it was. "Oh," he said, managing a smile. "Well, first things first, I guess."

Clarissa grabbed Freddie firmly by the arm and led him into the stairwell. She waited until a group of kids went by, then glared at him and said, "I am so mad at you, Freddie Ruiz. You know, I actually used to like you, can you believe it? Boy, was I wrong about you."

Freddie stood there frozen, unable to speak or move. Her sudden tirade had taken him completely by surprise.

"Why did you challenge Dondi to a race down Devil's Ravine?" she demanded. "Are you trying to get him killed or something? Huh? Come on, what do you have to say for yourself?"

"I didn't!" Freddie said, his voice cracking embarrassingly. "It was Dondi who challenged me!"

"Yeah, right. I believe that," she said with a derisive laugh. "You're the competitive one, not him. You challenged him on the halfpipe, and now this! Why don't you just give it a rest before somebody gets hurt?"

"I'm telling you!" Freddie pleaded. "It was Dondi who challenged me to Devil's Ravine! I know what he tells you about me, but you know what? It takes two to have a competition. And no matter what he told you, this was his idea." He stared intently at her. "I'm telling you the truth, Clarissa. Why don't you believe me? Can't you see I'm not lying?" He saw her gaze falter for an instant. "He lied to you, Clarissa," Freddie said. "I bet a lot of things he told you about me were lies."

Clarissa's eyes were darting around now, as if weighing what Freddie was saying. "Look, whatever," she finally said. "All I care about is that nobody gets hurt. You know what happened to Frank

117

Ritchie and those other two guys from the high school."

The two high school kids had broken their legs, and poor Frank Ritchie had spent six months in a coma. Freddie knew it, all right, and so did Dondi.

"You're saying you're not the competitive one. Well then, why don't you be the mature one and just back down? You know he never will."

Freddie couldn't breathe. Here was the girl he really, really liked, telling him to back out! If he did, would she like him better than Dondi?

She was right about one thing, anyway — Dondi would never back down. It showed Freddie that Clarissa had learned something about Dondi. Maybe she'd noticed other things, too.

"Promise me you'll at least *try* to stop it!" she begged. "I'm really scared somebody's going to get hurt."

Freddie swallowed hard. "I'll try," he said in a near whisper. "I promise."

"Thank you," she said, giving him a warm smile that gave Freddie goose bumps. He stood there frozen as she went up the stairs.

She'd said she was afraid someone would get hurt.

Someone — not necessarily Dondi. She'd even said she'd once liked him a lot!

He would have loved to stop the race, to please her. But how in the world was he going to do that without proving himself a loser, once and forever?

It was a cold, gray morning, and snow was coming. "You boys sure you want to go boarding today?" Esteban asked as he pulled the car into the parking lot at Snowshoe. "It's pretty miserable out."

"That's okay, Papi," Dondi said hurriedly. "Hey, Mami said you're up for a job, right?"

"Keep your fingers crossed," Esteban said with a little smile. He crossed his own fingers and held them up. "It's looking good so far. But nobody's offered me anything yet."

"Well then, pretty soon you'll be able to pay for my new board, right?" Dondi asked playfully.

Esteban reached over and tousled Dondi's long hair. "You're a wise guy, you know that?" he said. "A real wise guy." He turned to glance at Freddie.

"Really? You sure you want to go boarding? It's cold and windy, and snow's coming any minute."

Freddie nodded, unsmiling. "Mm-hmm" was all he said.

"You two guys are really crazy. Okay, I'll pick you up at four!"

As the boys got out and the car pulled away, Freddie could barely contain his sense of dread. He looked around for Nate and Brad. "Where are they?" he asked Dondi. "Maybe they decided not to come."

"They'll be here, don't worry," Dondi replied, avoiding his brother's eyes. A car turned in to the lot. "There they are. We're doing this, squirt. You asked for it, you got it. I'm going to show you who's the man."

"You're the one who asked for it!" Freddie argued. But Dondi wasn't listening. He was already slapping five with Nate and Brad, who were getting out of the car.

"What'd you tell your dad?" Nate asked Dondi after the car had pulled away.

"That we were going on the intermediate slope," Dondi replied.

"Good. Let's go."

The four boys took the chair lift to the top of the intermediate slope. Then, when the staff wasn't looking, they shoved off into the woods.

The ground was fairly level and they had no trouble making their way into the trees until they were out of sight and earshot. "It's over this way," Nate said. "Got to walk from here." They all took off their boards and followed him deeper into the woods.

Soon they came to a wooden hurricane fence that had a sign saying NO TRESPASSING: STATE FOREST, DEVIL'S RAVINE PRESERVE.

"This is it," Nate said. He and Brad bent the fence down and the four boys tramped over it, onto forbidden ground. "It's just on the other side of that ridge there."

"Man," Brad said as they got closer. "I can't believe I'm doing this again. This is so cool!"

He and Nate cast sly glances at Freddie and Dondi, then grinned broadly. "You guys are as nuts as we are!" Nate said.

"Yeah," Dondi said, managing a cocky grin. "Don't get your hopes up, though — the squirt here hasn't done anything yet."

"Neither have you, you jerk," Freddie said quickly.

Dondi turned and gave him a look. "Let's just go," he said, his jaw set.

When they reached the top of the ridge and looked down, even Nate and Brad turned serious. Below them, Devil's Ravine slid sharply away, twisting and turning, narrower than any ski slope Freddie had ever seen.

"Whoa," Dondi breathed. "That is steep."

"Wicked steep," Nate agreed. "That's why it's so much fun, man. You still gonna do it?"

"Uh-huh," Dondi said, his voice suddenly hesitant. "But maybe Freddie shouldn't . . ."

"What are you talking about?" Freddie muttered. "If anyone can't handle it, it's you. I'm way better than you, and you know it."

Dondi didn't say anything.

All four of them stared down the mouth of the ravine. To get to the bottom safely, they would have to run a narrow gauntlet over three blind jumps and past several trees that jutted out right in their path. The steep slope meant they'd be doing all this at top speed. Freddie swallowed hard. It was even worse than he'd imagined.

He thought of Frank Ritchie, who'd banged his head on one of those trees and wound up in a coma. Would the safety helmet he wore protect him from something like that? He thought of Eric in his wheelchair. And then he looked at Dondi.

Suddenly, a wave of misery hit Freddie, rising up from somewhere in his stomach and threatening to overwhelm him. Long-forgotten images of Dondi and himself, playing as toddlers and then as elementary schoolers, flooded his mind. He remembered that he had loved Dondi so much . . . idolized him . . . and he remembered what that love felt like. He felt it right now.

He had to do something. Something to stop this madness. But what?

"Okay, who goes first?" Brad asked, fidgeting nervously. "Any volunteers?"

"You guys should go first," Dondi said. "You know this slope. We'll watch you and learn from your mistakes."

"We're not gonna make any, man," Nate said, patting Dondi on the arm. "Okay, I'll go first. See you guys down there — one way or another!" He winked, turned, and shoved off into his run.

Freddie held his breath as Nate gathered speed. Even as Nate threw himself into his turns, cutting his edges crisp and sharp into the snow, Freddie was sure he was going to wipe out. From where they were standing, they could see Nate's first blind jump. Nate screamed as he went airborne, lost his balance, and nearly fell landing it. He barely managed to right himself in time to avoid a jutting tree limb in his path. Then he was out of sight for about thirty seconds, coming into view at the very bottom. Freddie knew there'd been two other blind jumps during those thirty seconds.

Nate seemed okay, though he was windmilling his arms to keep his balance. He skidded to a stop, turned, and waved his cap at them. Seconds later, they heard the triumphant whoop echoing up the mountainside.

"My turn," Brad said. "Hey, if I die, give me a big funeral, okay?" He grinned — a little uncertainly, Freddie thought — and then he too was gone.

Brad was as good a boarder as Nate and had had the benefit of watching Nate go first. Still, he too faltered during the first blind jump, and actually slid out for a moment before managing to get up again — and not a second too soon as he narrowly missed a tree branch.

Freddie doubted he could make it safely to the bottom. He knew Dondi couldn't.

"Y-you go first," Dondi said. His face was white as a sheet.

Freddie didn't move.

"You going or not?" Dondi said. "Do I have to go first?"

"No!" Freddie shouted.

"So go, then," Dondi said, motioning with his hand.

"You really want me to go?" Freddie asked.

Dondi stared at him, his face twitching. Freddie saw his own fear reflected in his brother's face. "I — I don't —"

"Come on, you wimps!" Nate's voice hollered up the ravine at them.

"*Buck-buck-buck-caw!*" Brad called out in his best chicken voice. "Come on, it's nothing!"

"Get down here!"

Dondi's face tightened, and he blinked back the tears. "That's it," he said. "I can't take this anymore. I'm going!"

"No, wait!" Freddie shouted. "Wait — I'll go first."

Dondi stared deep into his eyes. "You sure?" he asked.

"I'm sure," Freddie said.

"I don't know . . ."

"It's okay, Dondi. Don't worry about me. I'll be okay."

The idea had come to him at the last minute, as they stood there listening to the taunts from below. Suddenly, Freddie had seen a possible way out.

The only problem was, he was going to have to fall. And any fall here could be dangerous. But what had occurred to Freddie was this: If he could fake a fall, right near the top of the ravine, before he'd gotten to top speed, he might be able to escape injury and still stop this madness. Dondi would have to come help him, and then the two of them could safely leave the ravine. It would be a blow to Freddie's boarding reputation, but it was better than copping out completely. It was his only chance.

"Wish me luck, Dondi," he said.

"I do. Good luck," Dondi said, squeezing Freddie's shoulder.

And then Freddie was off and running. He kept

looking for a way to fall that looked real enough to fool the others. But this ravine was tricky, and before he knew it he was at the first blind jump!

"Yaaaaaa!" Freddie screamed as he went airborne. In that moment, time seemed to stretch out in front of him. He was high in the air, much higher than he'd ever been. There was the ground way beneath him, and he was still in perfect balance!

He knew in that moment that he could do this run, that he could get to the bottom safely. But could Dondi? He doubted it. He had only one chance to save his brother.

As he landed, Freddie let his back leg buckle. He went into a skid, throwing snow into a cloud all around him. A jutting tree limb zipped by him, and Freddie grabbed for it, using it to break his fall. It slowed him down enough that he came to a stop against a boulder, facedown in the snow. Had he not caught hold of the limb, the boulder might have crushed his skull, helmet or no helmet.

"Freddie!" he heard Dondi shouting from above him. "Are you all right?"

Freddie did his best acting job. "Aaaahhhhhh!

Owww! Help!" he yelled at the top of his lungs. "Dondi! Heeelllp! My leg . . ."

"I'm coming, little brother!" Dondi called. Looking from his prone position in the snow, Freddie could see Dondi coming, flailing his way through the deep snow. His board was stuck in a drift behind him.

Soon he was there. Freddie moaned as if he were dying. Dondi knelt down beside him. "Are you hurt bad?" he asked.

"I . . . don't know," Freddie gasped, wincing in pain for all he was worth.

"This was a stupid idea. And it's all my fault. I don't know why I dared you. I'm sorry, Freddie." Dondi's voice was cracking with emotion. "You're gonna be okay, right? Promise me you'll be okay. Oh, man, I can't believe this!"

"Not . . . all your fault," Freddie gasped in exaggerated pain. "It takes two. I . . . could have backed out or never taken you up on that stupid challenge."

"There's a lot of things neither of us should have done. Like I shouldn't have horned in on Clarissa when I knew you liked her." He shook his head and sighed. "Come on, little brother," he said, hoisting

Freddie up. He wrapped one arm around his brother, grabbed the snowboard with his free hand, and started trudging slowly back up the hill. "Let's get you some help right away."

Freddie let Dondi support him, and every once in a while let out a moan or a yelp of pain. His leg really did hurt a little, now that the shock of the fall had worn off. But it could have been a lot worse, he knew, both for him and for Dondi.

"Hey!" Nate's voice rang out from far below. "What happened?"

"Freddie got hurt!" Dondi yelled back. "We're going home!"

There was no reply. Good, Freddie thought. There would be time to tell them the story later. For now, he let himself relax against Dondi's firm grasp and focused on putting one foot in front of the other without stumbling.

In his mind's eye, he saw his father smiling at him, and sighed contentedly. Freddie had kept his word. He had been a good brother when it counted the most.

They came out of the woods near the entrance to Snowshoe's parking lot. "I'll call Papi to come get us," Dondi said, fishing for change in his pocket.

"No," Freddie said. "You go back and get your board. I'll call Papi."

Dondi looked at him. "What are you going to tell him?" he asked.

"Just that I fell on the slopes, of course," Freddie said. "Think I want him to know where we really were? Now go, I'll be fine here."

"Yeah?" Dondi searched his eyes, trying to tell whether Freddie really meant it.

"Yeah, I'll be all right," Freddie said. "I don't think anything's broken. I'll just be . . . limping around for a while, that's all." He limped over to the phone, as

131

if to prove his point. "You go ahead and get the board. Go on, go."

Still Dondi stood there, shifting from one foot to the other. "I guess you didn't do so good in the big-brother sweepstakes, did you?" he asked finally, avoiding Freddie's eyes.

"I did okay," Freddie said sincerely. "Sometimes brothers fight, that's all. We're no different than anybody else."

"Only more so, huh?" Dondi asked. He grinned conspiratorially.

"Yeah," Freddie agreed with a laugh. "Extreme sibling rivalry, a new Olympic sport."

Dondi laughed with him, then turned back to get his snowboard. Freddie called their dad, and half an hour later they were all riding home together.

Freddie and Dondi had figured out a whole story to tell about how Freddie got hurt, but it really wasn't necessary. Esteban didn't even notice that Freddie was limping, he was so excited.

"Guess what, you guys?" he asked his sons. "Your old man got the job! How do you like that?"

"Papi, that's great!" Freddie said.

"Finally, at long last!" Dondi chimed in, saying the wrong thing as usual.

But this time, it didn't seem to bother Esteban. "It sure took long enough, didn't it?" he agreed cheerfully. "But this is a really good situation, great salary and bonuses — Mami's going to be able to go back to regular hours, how do you like that?"

"Yessss!" Dondi said exultantly. "We get Mami-cooked meals again!"

"Your cooking was okay, Papi," Freddie assured him.

"Yeah, right," Esteban said, mimicking his sons' way of talking. "That's me — the magic microwaving heat-'n'-eat chef!"

They were all so excited by the time they got home that Freddie forgot to limp when he got out of the car.

Dondi noticed immediately. "Hey, you're cured already?" he asked, surprised.

"N-no," Freddie said hurriedly, his eyes avoiding Dondi's suddenly suspicious gaze. "I'm just . . . toughing it out in front of Papi, that's all."

"Hmmm," Dondi said, regarding him doubtfully.

"I guess you've got bones made out of rubber, huh?"

"Yeah, that's me," Freddie agreed with a smile. "Good old rubber bones." He followed Dondi into the house, limping just a little, wondering if Dondi had caught on to his game — and if he had, whether he would play along.

"So you deliberately tanked your run?" Steve was incredulous. "I can't believe it!"

"I had to," Freddie explained between bites of the mystery meat that was Monday's school lunch. "It was the only way out."

"Wait a minute," Eric objected. "First of all, you could have been killed. Second of all, you could have been killed."

"Could not," Freddie protested weakly. "I can make that run anytime."

"Sure you can," Eric said sarcastically. "So could I. So could Steve here. But the point is —"

"The point is, it worked," Freddie interrupted. "Dondi gets to be the big hero, and I get to save him from hurting himself. Nobody's calling anybody a wimp. In fact, both of us get credit for having the guts to even go up there. So what's the problem?"

"Start with having to limp around and wear that Ace bandage for weeks," Steve said. "I can't believe you're going to all this trouble just to make your brother look good. That is so bizarre!"

"I have to," Freddie said, "but I won't be limping for long. I'll say it healed fast. By Wednesday, it's over, that's it."

"What's the purple and green stuff, fake bruises?" Steve asked.

"Yeah. My mom's eyeshadow. It looks pretty gross, doesn't it?" Freddie asked with a grin.

Eric shook his head in admiration. "I guess it wasn't too bad a plan at that," he said. "Better than going ahead with it, and better than getting laughed at for the rest of your life. Pretty clever after all. Congratulations."

"And don't ever do it again!" Steve cautioned. "We wouldn't want to lose you."

"Man, I'm never going near that place again!" Freddie said with a chuckle. "You should have seen it, with all the snow and rocks and trees. Whoo!"

"Hey, klutzo!" Nate Sherman came over to their

135

table, followed by Brad Forest. "How's the leg? Can I sign your cast?"

"It's not broken, it's just a bad bruise."

"Aw, did the itty-bitty baby fall down and get a boo-boo?" Brad joked. He and Nate cracked up, slapping each other on the back.

"He's not a baby, you morons!" It was Dondi, pushing his way between them. "He only fell because he's on a brand-new board and it's a slicker ride than he's used to." He nodded at Freddie. "He's better than either of you were when you were twelve years old. Give him a break, huh? Besides, he's got guts — you've got to give him that."

"More than you, Dondi boy," Nate said. "I notice you conveniently didn't have to go down the ravine."

"Oh, because I took time out to help my little brother, I'm a wimp now?" Dondi asked, a challenge in his voice. "You want to just come out and say it? Because we can take it outside."

"Don't fight, Dondi," Freddie intervened. "They're not worth it. They're just being the jerks they are. They can't help themselves."

"Shut up, you punk!" Brad said, reaching for Freddie.

Dondi grabbed his arm and thrust it away. "Hey!" he warned. "That's my little brother. You mess with him, you have to deal with me!"

"Man, forget it," Nate told Brad, leading him away. "Leave them alone. Facts are facts — we're still the only ones to get down Devil's Ravine in one piece."

"Yeah!" Brad agreed, and the two exchanged high-fives and contemptuous glances at Freddie and Dondi.

After they had gone, Freddie turned to Dondi and said, "Thanks. You stuck up for me. That was, well, unbelievable."

"Ah, forget it." Dondi looked embarrassed. "I just don't like people picking on my little brother. Anyway, I've got to go. See you." He moved off, and the younger boys sat watching him.

"Can you believe what we just saw?" Steve asked.

"I never thought I'd see the day," Eric agreed. "Well, I guess if there's hope for Dondi, maybe the world isn't going to end after all."

Freddie?"

Freddie had been getting his coat out of his locker. At the sound of Clarissa's voice he felt his heart begin to race. He spun around and found her standing only a foot or so away, smiling at him.

"Oh, hi, Clarissa," he said, hoping he wasn't flushing as red as he thought he was. "How're you doing?"

"Fine. I heard about what happened Saturday." Her face grew serious.

"Oh. That. Yeah, well . . ." He looked down at his sneakers. He knew Dondi must have told her that Freddie had chickened out. She probably thought he was a total coward, on top of all the other stuff she already believed about him.

"I just wanted to say thank you," she said softly.

He looked up and met her gaze. "Huh?"

"For what you did. For not letting Dondi get hurt."

"But I —"

"I know you faked getting hurt," she said. "I think that was so great of you."

"How did you —?" But he already knew how she knew. Dondi must have told her. And if he had, it meant that Dondi also knew the truth. It meant Dondi had been glad to get out of it too.

"Freddie," Clarissa said, "I want you to know I'm sorry. I was wrong about you. You're not immature like I thought. So" — and here she smiled — "want to go to the movies with me? As friends?"

Freddie was stunned. "I, uh . . . sure," he finally managed. "But . . . what about Dondi?"

"Oh," Clarissa said, sighing. "I like Dondi and all, but I don't think I really want to date him — or anybody, if you want to know the truth. There'll be plenty of time for that sort of stuff when I'm older. Right now, there's just one new thing I want to do. Dondi told me to ask you about it."

Freddie waited, suddenly wary. What could Dondi possibly have told Clarissa now?

Clarissa laughed. "Don't look so suspicious! It's just that I've never snowboarded before, but it sure looks like fun. Do you think maybe you could —?"

"Give you lessons?" Freddie finished, his voice almost cracking with glee. "Absolutely!"

"Outstanding," she said. "How about Saturday, before the movie?"

"Cool," he said, smiling and nodding. "You're going to love snowboarding."

Freddie stood there in the hallway watching her go, not even noticing the other kids passing by. He was sitting on top of his own little world, and he didn't care who knew it.

"Lean into it! No! Ahhh! Look out!" Freddie shouted, laughing as Clarissa tumbled into the snow again. He tramped over to her and helped her up again. She wobbled and slid, and the two of them went down in a heap in the snow.

"Whoo-hoo! Watch it, you two, people are going to start talking!"

They both sat bolt upright. Dondi was standing at

the foot of the bunny slope, laughing and clapping his hands in amusement.

"Dondi, cut it out!" Freddie yelled.

"Uh-oh, he's gonna beat me up! Help! Help, somebody! A little peanut is gonna beat me up!"

"That's it!" Freddie got to his feet and started running toward Dondi.

"Okay, okay, put your dukes up!" Dondi called out, laughing hysterically as Freddie slipped and fell in the snow at Dondi's feet. "Whoa! He's down for the count, ladies and gentlemen!"

Freddie reached out and grabbed Dondi's leg, pulling him down to the ground. The two boys tussled playfully, throwing stage punches at each other and grimacing in mock pain.

"Ow! Mami, Mami, it hurts!" Dondi said in a high baby voice. "Do your worst, fool — I'm still a better snowboarder than you."

"Dream on," Freddie said, grunting with the effort of pinning Dondi down.

"You're teaching her wrong," Dondi gasped as Freddie started to tickle him. "You'd better let me do it."

"Make yourself scarce, Dondi!"

"Would you guys please stop killing each other?" Clarissa called out. "I need some help here. I've fallen, and I can't get up!"

Dondi stood up and brushed the snow off his pants and coat. "I would have beaten you that time, squirt, if the little lady hadn't rescued you. And you know it, admit it!"

"Never! One good punch and you would have been out like a light!" Freddie retorted.

With a final laugh, Dondi picked up his board and headed toward the chair lift. Freddie turned to help Clarissa up.

"I guess Dondi and I are always going to be competing," Freddie said, sighing. "I know you think it's pretty immature."

"Actually, what I just saw didn't look like two guys competing — not really, anyway," Clarissa said. "That's not the way you guys used to fight."

"Yeah, it is," Freddie corrected her. "A long time ago, we used to do it that way. It was fun." He smiled at the memory. "Well, maybe we can get it back, huh?"

"I know you can," said Clarissa. "Now, come on. I want to try this again." She grabbed her snowboard and started walking back up to the top of the bunny slope.

Freddie took one last look at Dondi's retreating figure. Dondi turned at that moment, gave Freddie the thumbs-up sign. Freddie smiled, returned it, and headed up the slope after Clarissa. "We're brothers, after all," he said to himself.

Inside his head, he could see his father's eyes smiling at him.

READ ALL THE BOOKS
In The
New MATT CHRISTOPHER Sports Library!

CATCH THAT PASS!
978-1-59953-105-2

CENTER COURT STING
978-1-59953-106-9

DIRT BIKE RACER
978-1-59953-113-7

ICE MAGIC
978-1-59953-112-0

THE KID WHO ONLY HIT HOMERS
978-1-59953-107-6

LONG ARM QUARTERBACK
978-1-59953-114-4

MOUNTAIN BIKE MANIA
978-1-59953-108-3

SKATEBOARD TOUGH
978-1-59953-115-1

SNOWBOARD MAVERICK
978-1-59953-116-8

SNOWBOARD SHOWDOWN
978-1-59953-109-0

SOCCER HALFBACK
978-1-59953-110-6

SOCCER SCOOP
978-1-59953-117-5